OTHER BOOKS
BY GINA BERRIAULT

The Descent
Conference of Victims
The Infinite Passion of Expectation
The Mistress
The Son

# THE
# LIGHTS
# OF
# EARTH

*A Novel by*

*Gina
Berriault*

1984

NORTH POINT PRESS · SAN FRANCISCO

The author thanks the John Simon Guggenheim Foundation
for the time to complete this novel.

"A tremendous passion is this longing that our memory may be rescued from the oblivion which overtakes others."

Miguel de Unamuno

# THE LIGHTS OF EARTH

# 1

Years after the night of that strange little party her memory played a trick on her. Her memory set him among the others, the guest of honor who heard every word, who saw every gesture and every expression on every face. But he wasn't there. He wasn't even expected that night. He must have been still in Spain or New York or down in Los Angeles or over the continent on his way back to San Francisco. He must have been up in the sky, somewhere over all, as the suddenly famous ones seem to be.

The name of the couple whose house it was, the house where she had not been before and was never to enter again, seemed of no consequence and she didn't quite hear it. Later, when she knew the name of the wife, she was unable to say that name aloud. An ordinary name to anyone else, for her it was the shattering presence of the woman herself. The couple had asked Claud, a friend of Martin—the guest of honor who wasn't there—to bring Ilona along. Just by her presence and even without a word she might tell them something about the man who was her lover. Even though he was to appear soon, any day, their impatience threw open the door to her as wide as it would have been had he accompanied her. They must have been hoping for someone like him to come into their lives, each one's hope so ardently secret from the other that he must have seemed inevitable.

The oval glass in the oak door of the Victorian house was etched so profusely with grapes and leaves and tendrils it served as an impenetrable silver mist that with utmost graciousness denied you a view of what went on inside. A lamp or a chandelier in some far room glinted off the entwined grapes and turned them gold, now one and now another, a matter of how you shifted your feet or your eyes.

Claud had ridiculed the host on the way over, but now at the last moment the desire to be presentable forced him to comb down his hair, tossed by the wind. He wore a sportcoat with only one button missing and each pocket held a pack of cigarettes to protect him from his perverse need to smoke the couple's. Ilona had refused at first to come along. She had come only because the couple's curiosity about the man who was her lover stirred her own curiosity about something she wanted not to think about at all—a premonition of loss.

Grasping Claud's arm, shaking Ilona's right hand with his left, the host drew them inside, the three awkwardly linked. The host's jeans were faded, his hiking boots were grayed by rough use, and the most humble garment of all was his gauzy shirt from India. In those years, the early seventies, some affluent young were imitating the poor of the world. The shirt, however, failed to lessen his chest's prosperity. It was as obdurate as all other wealthy chests, narrow or broad, that she'd slipped by or asked something of, a job or simple directions, or brought something to, a tray of whatever was ordered.

Beyond the wide doorway to the dining room, the several persons lounging around the long table were like actors on a stage, made small by their surroundings and each striving to be seen and heard. Except one, who had no need to strive—the one among the women who was beautiful, and Ilona knew at once that the woman was the wife of the man who was guiding Claud and herself toward the table and knew that she was the eventual one, the one who takes away the lover, the one who is a reward in a time of rewards, and she wished for herself a time when presentiment of loss would never bother her because she would be wise enough to know that loss was as natural as breathing.

Ilona, seated across from the woman, looked instead at the couple's son, close to three years old, who sat elevated by cushions next to his mother, turning his gaze from one face to another, bending over his plate to see who was speaking at the end of the table, to see who was laughing. The little boy bore his resemblance to his mother like a gift whose value he knew about. His eyes, like his mother's, seemed balanced by serenity, by the trust that all he was to desire of life would be granted, and Ilona called upon reason to rescue her from her archaic view of the world that saw it divided between those who appeared to be blessed and those who appeared to be forsaken, and reason failed. She tried then to imagine at this table a great writer of the past, say a century ago, someone who had observed compassionately women who went unnoticed, but if that figure, whoever he was, were really to be at this table, absorbed again in life, his gaze would be on the beautiful wife, amazingly like a woman who had enthralled him a hundred years ago.

The host at the head of the table was accusing his guests of envy, envy of the man somewhere up in the air. "Severe envy. It's worse than hepatitis. More people die of it. Nausea, insomnia. But the worst symptom is impotence."

6

"You know that for a fact?" someone asked, and someone else laughed.

"Impotence," the host repeated. "Of the mind. Of the hand that holds your very own little pen. Look at Claud. Claud hasn't written one word in ten years and he'd like you to think he couldn't care less, he's through. But look. Overnight his hair's turned white and the whites of his eyes have turned green. Claud, let everybody see your eyes."

Claud was smiling, smoking a cigarette of his own. His hair was as dark as ever and his eyes as clear as they ever were. "If I'm dying it's not from envy. It's from what that Frenchman, Péguy, said—You die of your whole life. Not just one shock."

The host brought up a *Time* from under his chair, already open to the photograph of the absent guest of honor, and held up the magazine for all to see. Ilona had read the review weeks ago and the other guests must also have read it then, but everybody complyingly raised their eyes. Except the wife, who was placing tidbits from her own plate onto her son's plate, while the child gazed up anxiously at the picture, afraid of missing something so important to his father.

"One of those faces that haven't been lived in yet," the host said. "He's thirty-four and he looks nineteen and he'll look nineteen when he's ninety, God help him."

"I think . . ." A girl, afraid to contest with the host, appeared to be talking to her plate. "I think he deserves all the praise he's been getting."

Down came the magazine, down beside his plate, and his hand came down flat on the small picture. "I agree, I agree. That's why I've called you all together. To sing his praises. We'll practice every night, we'll gather here every night, and the night he walks in the door a heavenly choir shall greet him."

Like falsely obedient children who've bested a parent they took up their forks and wineglasses again, complacently silent. When the array of delicatessen delights on each plate was one or two bites less, the chatter began again—nothing about the novel itself but everything about those persons who were welcoming Martin Vandersen into the world: critics, and the movie producer who had bought the screen rights to the novel, and the director at whose villa on the Costa del Sol Martin had been a guest, and the actor who was sought for the lead. "Sought," cried the host, staring wildly upward. "One lousy actor *sought* like in 'they sought God,' like in 'they sought justice.' " But though they pleasurably interrupted one another with details about the lives of those legendary persons who were surrounding Martin at this birth, they appeared to be baffled over why they were so affected by somebody else's recognition, somebody else's entry into the light. She saw the bafflement in their eyes and heard it in their voices.

Out in the living room the host sat down at Ilona's feet,

took off his boots, and attempted the lotus position. Apart from them, the others were talking loudly and his wife was upstairs, putting the child to bed.

"She had a lover in Italy last year," he said, low. "A good man. A fine sculptor. American, living in Florence. We would have been great friends if he hadn't been her lover. Your Martin reminds me of him. I met Martin a couple of days before he left, ran into him and Claud, and his resemblance to her last year's lover was remarkable. The looks, the wit." His glance slipped sideways on its way up to her face. "What's he like? I mean when you get to know him."

Bearing a tray of decanters and goblets, his wife came into the room, and the question seemed asked for her. They would have to answer the question themselves, each with a secret answer.

The man at her feet rocked back and forth, gripping his ankles. "How long have you known him?"

"Oh, four years." The number of years for lovers was supposed to mean something, a measurement of depth or truth, but numbers were revelations only for scientists. The things she knew about the lovers she'd never tell this man, and one was that love was never certain—who but herself thought it could be?—but that under the uncertainty of love lay the certainty of comradeness. What else wouldn't she tell? That when Martin had reminded her a time was to come when he would be elsewhere, she had listened reasonably and amenably, but they had pained her, those reminders, and once, afraid that if their time together was without love it was a wasted time, she had gone so far as to quote Camus. "You enrich the future by giving all to the present." Because she disparaged her own words, because her own words lacked persuasion, she relied on time-honored words. After that heavy-laden quote he gave up his warnings and reminders, convinced at last that she knew about endings and about elsewhere.

Massaging his calves as though easing a cramp, he asked, "Ah, you live together?"

"Yes, we live together." Her answer appeared to soothe him, he seemed to accept it as assurance that they would continue to live together and his wife and himself also continue to live together, with no outside interference. "Though sometimes we lived apart."

The man at her feet knew very little, probably, about makeshift dwellings that weren't your own and that convinced you of a destiny to be always without possessions and never even to desire them. So he might be unable to see that the way they lived together was another bond that made them kindred even apart. Six weeks ago, when Martin was in Spain or somewhere in Europe, the house across the bay, in the little town at the foot of the mountain, the house where they had lived together with her child, was sold, and she had found a small apartment in the city, hoping that when Martin returned they would find a larger one together.

"Claud tells me Martin used to live in a basement out by the ocean. Claud says the house was riddled with termites and their eggs or turds rained down on your friend's manuscripts. He said that in the flat upstairs the fleas were like a living carpet and when Martin went up there once to use the phone the fleas were all over him as soon as he stepped inside. He turned and ran."

Any creature, she thought, no matter how microscopically small, that's on or near a person who's become famous, becomes famous also.

"Claud says Martin had only two plates and he put the cooking pot on the table. Claud says he kept his manuscripts in a grocery box and a mouse made herself a nest in there and gave birth, and he didn't know it and kept piling up the pages." A pause. "Was it deliberate? I mean, was it a show of poverty, like 'See, I was poor and now I deserve the rewards'?"

"It was what you call necessary poverty," she said. If it *was* an attempt at saintly asceticism so that when recognition came along nobody would want to deny him its rewards, she didn't want to know about it. She didn't want to know his superstitions, just as she didn't want to know her own. Superstitions were too much to know about anyone and yourself.

"Claud says they've torn down the house and put up a motel. Too bad. What they should have done—the city, I mean, or the state, or even the federal government—was buy the house, restore it, and put up a bronze plaque that says Martin Vandersen lived here, and the dates. If they'd only known. And turn the basement into a museum. The pot and the two plates on the table, a stuffed mouse in the manuscripts, the bed made, the covers turned back like he's away on a journey but he's coming home any day now. You've seen pictures of Tolstoy's study? Everything just where it was when the great man died."

If Martin were present, and if she were to take him aside and point out to him this man's fear of him, this ridicule in the guise of praise, then Martin, who wanted never to suspect anybody, would say *What's there to fear about me?*

Over across the blue Persian carpet the wife was pouring brandy, and Ilona saw again how each particular of beauty, the beauty of any person, of any object, of anything on earth or in the heavens, leads you on, mesmerized, to all particulars, and she saw again how a woman's beauty seems to pardon that woman in advance for any betrayal, any transgression, for grief brought to others.

"If he's got no place to go," the man at her feet was saying, "he can stay with us until he finds a place. Plenty of room here," pointing heavenward. "Come on, I'll show you," leaping up, leaving his boots behind.

Climbing the stairs at his side, she saw how eager his feet in socks appeared, eager to run and prepare the way for an invasion of his privacy by the man up in the night sky.

On the middle floor they passed the half-open door of the master bedroom and she kept herself from glancing in. She might glance in on her way down. When you were on your way down you were already on your way out, like a trespasser discovered in the upper regions.

Gently he pushed the door to the boy's room a bit more open, motioning for her to step just inside and no farther. The child in the large bed, the lamp with its rosy shade, the shadows—it was like a very large oil painting with somebody in it preciously small.

"Does he resemble me?"

She had seen no resemblance at the table. It was as if the mother and the child had requested the artist to leave the father out of the picture.

"He isn't mine, you know." A pause. "You know about it? His father was Joseph Neely, the poet. They'd run away. He died of a heart attack in Greece, on one of those idyllic islands. She was in a terrible state. Grief, you know, and pregnant, and I went there. We cried together. My God, we held each other and cried for a whole day and a night." His hoarse whisper, his feet in socks—he was like a trespasser himself.

Up another flight, the last staircase uncarpeted, and the room they entered at the back of this floor contained only a narrow bed, a straight-back chair, a small table. No rug, no shade over the ceiling globe.

13

"If he lived that way in his basement he'll like this room the way it is. We haven't got to it yet. We'll find him some termites if they'll make him feel at home."

Was he expecting the guest to stay forever? Years later, when one evening she was passing through this neighborhood, the house that she did not want to identify for certain in the row of stolid and stately houses caught her eye and roused up again the emotions of that time of loss. The host's expectation of a guest who would stay on and on had been fulfilled. The house had become the guest's, though the guest wasn't there anymore and the couple and the child weren't there and the house belonged to somebody else.

Restlessly he moved around the room, a host expecting one last guest before the festivities can begin, and she thought: He throws open all doors and begs loss to enter. Had he brought her into this almost bare room so that she might give him evidence in advance, just by her presence, of how his life was to be changed by the guest who would soon be lying in the narrow bed, sitting down with them to their meals, reclining on their couches, lying in their tub? The guest might even play the grand piano downstairs, an accomplished musician, or he might be a raconteur whose every word was given rapt attention. Once you leaped out of obscurity so many talents came to light.

Awkwardly, as though stricken by shame, he faced her from a corner. "You know I write myself? Claud must have told you. That's my study, the other door."

14

Was he waiting for her to ask him what his novel was about? She never asked that question of anyone and side-stepped it when it was asked of her, and even if he were pleased to answer she chose not to see in his eyes, as he told her, all that pleading with reality to yield up its meanings.

"It's about them," he said. "It's about this poet who runs off with somebody's wife and it's no bed of roses. Some of them die of joy after twenty years but some of them, like Neely, drop off fast even though she's doing all she can to make him the happiest man in the world. It might have been too much for his heart, he might have wanted to be free of what he'd wanted so much." He glanced at her sharply to see if he were truly heard. "She doesn't know what my novel's about, she thinks it's about my childhood in Iran. My father was an oil exec. I tell her Scheherazade tales and she thinks that's what it's all about. Something else she doesn't know and that's the guilt I feel, stuck in that room like I'm in solitary for committing some crime, and the crime is what I'm doing in there. I'm not supposed to touch them, I'm not supposed to get all wound up in it. It's like I've been warned to leave them alone. In other words, leave life alone. Die of it if you want to, but don't presume to know how it is with anybody else."

He came toward her so fast, switching off the light so fast, that she was forced to step aside to allow him to leave the room first.

On the way down she glanced into their bedroom. A lamp

was on and she saw a wide bed covered over with a pure white spread, she saw a deep red Oriental carpet and an antique chair draped with a black silk Spanish shawl. On the nights when their guest was to lie alone, up there on the top floor, would he know that the woman lying beside her husband longed to lie beside him, instead? Ilona, glancing in, was reminded of herself at twelve, when every night before sleep she imagined a different being for herself from head to foot, and that fervent concentration on every particular (from an actress up on the screen—her eyes; from a girl in school—her mouth; from a woman passed on the street—her hair) was to bring about a miracle. When she woke up in the morning she'd be the girl she'd created the night before. The woman who was embraced in that broad bed, the woman loved by many men—was she someone whom the girl, Ilona, would have chosen to become, back on those nights of dreaming herself up?

When they came down the last stairs and the room with its company was out before them, she was still in the past, the street urchin with the tangled hair and torn dress and the shame over herself, the child gazing at the scene through a window, not wanting in, only wondering why so much light, why so many things reflecting light—silver and mirrors and glass and jewels and eyes—were always on the other side of the pane. The wife looked up at them and seemed to know all that her husband had told Ilona, and the

face of the woman imprinted itself in her memory, an in-
fliction, a trial, a dazzling fact of life.

The host brought Ilona a cognac and she stood with the
other guests around him. He was lightly drunk, trans-
ported by his performance. "Old Fyodor, here's old Fyodor
back in Russia. Here he is, knocking his shins on heavy
Russian furniture again. He's just come back from the gambling spas, Baden-Baden, linden trees, fountains, roulette
wheels, chandeliers like heavenly constellations over his little demented head, and here he is and he's under contract to
that swine."

"Paulina lay around naked," Claud interrupted. "She lay
around and wouldn't let him touch her. All across Europe.
The girl he went gambling with, he couldn't touch her."
And someone laughed, a short derisive laugh.

"Anna, I'm talking about Anna, the girl he married.
Anna comes after Paulina. I don't know what the hell happened to Paulina. Anna was his second wife. The first wife
was insane and then she died. You ever think how many of
the greats married insane women? Well, here he is, I'll start
over again. Here he is back in Russia and he's under contract
to that swine and he's got to hand over another novel or else
he forfeits his rights to all his works so far. He's got one
month and not one word."

Ilona saw that his wife had wandered away to the stereo
and, her back turned to the group, was selecting an album.

17

The low voice of a French male singer was heard, and the woman bowed her head to listen.

"One lousy month and not one word. Then this friend says he knows about this class where the girls are learning some sort of hieroglyphics that's just been invented. Shorthand? What the hell's that? So old Fyodor asks the instructor to send over a student, and he sends over this girl, twenty years old. . . . " One fast step to the side and he was the girl, gazing in awe at the space vacated by Fyodor. "Are you Mr. Dostoevski?" A girl's tremolo. Jumping back into Fyodor's space, he brought up from his chest a weary bass voice. "My dear Anna, I've got one month, my dear, one lousy month to get this novel together." Then he was himself again, his voice his own. "You ever see pictures of her? Tolstoy told her they were look-alikes, Fyodor and her. They were. You can see for yourself. Same eyes, same stare. Or her eyes got to imitating his, she was looking into them all the time. Anyway, she took it all down in hieroglyphics every day, and every night she went home to Mama. They got it all together. So old Fyodor—everybody was old at forty in those days—asked her to marry him. My God, she loved him for the rest of his life, even when he pawned the baby's shoes for gambling money."

Sweat shone on his face, he was a medium on the verge of collapse after conversing with that couple on the Other Side. His clownish act, his exertion stirred Ilona's sympathy. Was it his way of telling his wife that if only she would

18

stay by him, they too would be remembered by the world? Now that his performance was over, the seductively aloof voice of the French singer was heard by all.

When the guests were putting on their coats, the host, waving his arms, called for silence. "My friends, I'd like to sing a little song for you. It's a song composed especially for the remarkable man who was unable to be with us tonight because he's in demand everywhere else." With a rapturous voice he sang his variation of a song heard everywhere, "Mar-tin in the sky-eye with dia-monds," while everyone listened dutifully like children taught a song to sing together. Except his wife, who listened incuriously as if not listening.

It was then, at last, that her eyes met Ilona's—while her husband gazed up through the ceiling at the starry heavens and sang his one line—and Ilona saw the woman's awareness of *her*, she saw the other woman's curiosity about what she, Ilona, meant or had meant or would mean in the future to the man who was to appear any day now, any moment, out of the sky.

# 2

Claud caught at Ilona to keep himself from falling down the front steps. The collar of his coat was turned under, his hair, combed so carefully before he pressed the bell, was hanging in limp spirals, and his sight was hiding far inside like that of a nocturnal animal, a predator waiting for deeper night.

On the sidewalk—the lurch, the stagger, while she held his arm to keep him up. If she were to let go he might pitch forward onto his face. But out of sight of their host in the doorway and of the other guests, he was not so drunk for her as for them.

"My mother," he explained, "taught me manners. She said someday you're going to mingle with people who count. So tell them how much you enjoyed their company and they'll invite you back again. That's how I do it."

Except for the seething sound he made by whistling through his teeth and for the rattle under the floor of his car, the drive to their neighborhood was a silent one and careful. They lived a few blocks apart on the north side of a hill above the piers fanning out into the bay.

She had been in Claud's one-room place only with Martin, and when the three of them sat around in there, this man seemed not to see her. Something had changed at the party. He had come to stand by her or sit by her, and he had told her who the others were—that man, an attorney, that woman, a psychologist, that man, a reporter, and he had told her what he knew about them, especially their frailties, and from across the room he had saluted her, and the salute was a puzzling tribute. At last, this night, he was acknowledging her presence.

"Come on in," he said, "and I'll drink yours for the road."

She wanted to stay only a minute and to sit in the straight chair, but he swung that chair aside to give her access to the lumpy, upholstered armchair. He sat down on the bed, leaned over to set an ashtray on the floor between his feet, and stayed in that position to hide the troubling in his eyes.

He was an anonymous man again after the brief recognition for his own novel. She hadn't known him then—ten, twelve years ago—and if she were to have met him she would have lost her voice and run away, wanting not to be counted among all those asking something of someone in the light—*Oh, please see me*—asking the visible one to make them visible too. Usually now he was out in his old fishing boat, wherever the fish or his restlessness led him, and she remembered dawns when she stood at the window of the rickety house at the water's edge, over across the bay, the newborn girl in her arms, watching the fishing boats moving out toward the channel and the open sea, a line of dark imprints on the pearly, luminous waters, and she remembered thinking *It's not just a matter of a livelihood. They're testing to see if they're looked after, out there in deep water.*

It was cold in the room. The oven door hung open and some heat was coming out, but not far enough.

"It's a blow upside the head," he said, smacking his temple. "Fame hits you like that. That's how it hit me. Even my dinky fame compared to a very large fame. It's like a comic strip. Whack! The guy's out cold, he sees stars, he's got this silly smile on his face. What it did, it was like I was forgiven for everything in my life which I shouldn't have done and for all those things I didn't do which I ought to have done, just because my past, my life, was exactly as it ought to have been, because if I hadn't lived such a life I wouldn't have got

22

what I got, my dinky fame. It was proved to me that it's an all right world and God is an all right fellow. When I woke up I wiped that smile off my face. It made me look like those used car salesmen up on billboards, like those hearing-aid salesmen and realtors smiling away in the yellow pages of your phone book, like Orville Rednecker on his cartons of ice cream. I thought—Holy Asses! We all got ourselves some homemade immortality."

No matter what their host had said about envy, accusing all his guests, envy wasn't this man's problem and it wasn't her own and it might not be the host's. What was it then? Was it a storm warning when the horizon was clearer than it had ever been, the way they thought Martin Vandersen saw it now? Was it your own longing to be seen on earth while you were still here, and remembered for a while after? Was it only that longing, simple enough? Whatever it was, their host had called them together so that no one would be alone with it. Until now, after the party.

"Let's talk," he said, "about something cheerful. Do you ever think about the end of the world? You think I don't know why I like to think about it, but I know, I know. You've heard about that ecstatic feeling epileptics get before a fit? Well, say you're ecstatic over a friend's good fortune and then you throw a fit."

"Some other time," she said.

"By cataclysm," he began, "and the kind I'm talking about isn't what everybody else is talking about, like what

23

we're doing to the planet. I've got an Old Testament God hanging around in my head and it will be His doing. You've got Him, too. I can see it in your eyes, you always look like you're waiting for an angel to banish you from wherever you are. I was never raised in any religion and I never chose one for my very own, and a certain convert, my ex-wife, used to ask me How are you going to write about a tormented Catholic? And I told her I'll just consult the encyclopedia and find out all about a cathedral, where the hell the nave is or the apse, and then I'll throw him in and torment him. Well, this cataclysm is going to be our hothead God's when He's pissed-off enough. Say He gives a little push with His finger, say it's the same finger He touched Adam with, and the world somersaults. Over we go. The ocean goes bed-hopping. We'll all be swept over to the other side of the world and around again. It's not true you only go round once. Waves of unprecedented fury. If we could see it on television that's what they'd say. 'A wave of unprecedented fury is sweeping over the earth.' Then your set's off and you and yours are swept away the same moment as your anchor man. Fffft."

One foot was turned in, pigeon-toed. It was that way when he walked, too, as if part of him, if only a foot, was at odds with the sardonic rest. "If it happens tonight, if the earth somersaults tonight, you alone in your bed, me alone in mine, that'll take care of any trouble Martin might have caused us. Something bigger than Martin Vandersen will consume us."

## 3

Out alone in a neighborhood that was now her own but still unfamiliar, out alone in the night, she tried to free herself from the person she was with others, the trespasser who imagined more than she saw and saw more than she ought to see, the person who could not look into their eyes because, if she did, they would look into hers and find there the uninvited guest. She tried to rescue herself from this night, from the party, from the couple who lived in that house, from Claud, and from the premonition of loss, and the way to try was to remember two nights ago when she had embraced her daughter at the airport and watched the plane rise into the night sky.

Among a crowd of passengers checking their luggage, their unwieldy backpacks, she stood with her daughter, sixteen, Antonia, going off to Nepal, to the Himalaya, into antiquity. Not yet dawn, deep night still, and she had put her hands to her child's face and kissed her on the mouth, on the brow, on each cheek, and over again.

"Mother?"

"Yes?"

"All you need to do is bless me."

"I bless you."

"Now if you wake up in the night afraid about me, all you need to do is remember that you blessed me."

Only a few pinpoints of light—the plane was only that, and then the lights had disappeared fast, though she had tried to mistake a star for the plane. It had come as a surprise to her that her child, or anyone, believed that she could bless and that the blessing might work.

Ilona, climbing the hill, became someone other than the woman she had been at the party. Alone in the night she became the one she was in solitude, solaced by the delusion that simply because she was given life then some deep mystery was promised her, not any answers, only the experience of mystery, a beneficence unlike that granted to those beings who belonged on earth with ease.

A green globe hung above the narrow passageway that

led from the street into the concrete courtyard formed by old frame apartment buildings, where the wind rustled newspapers all night long into corners, and a large but dim globe burned above the flight of concrete stairs that led up from the courtyard, and only the night sky lit the higher flight of shaky, wooden stairs and the landing and her door.

# 4

Ilona, remembering how the wife had looked at her that last moment, remembered another moment four years ago when Martin's wife had come out into the night to see who Ilona was, to see who Ilona was in *his* eyes, divining her own future in Ilona's face.

It was in the time when he lived by the ocean and Ilona would drive across the bridge and through the city, out to the Great Highway where the houses facing the sea appeared shriveled by years of salt and wind, and the dim glow in their windows resembled small lights at sea, ready to disappear. At low tide she caught glimpses of the wide beach beyond the high sand dunes, and when the waves were heavy and close their sound against the rows of houses was like the ocean itself towering over them. He liked it there. Any hour, even in the middle of the night, he would leap up from his work and run along the strip of wet, hard sand, and sometimes she ran with him, over the mirrored sky, over the night clouds gliding along under her feet.

Always, when she was expected, his window lit the passage between the houses. His basement rooms were ground-level, once a garage. That night the passage was almost dark. Had she come when he wasn't expecting her, drawn only by her own desire? Once in a while, even when he seemed most grateful for her, another voice of his spoke up, cautioning her to expect a time when he was to be elsewhere, but she hadn't expected to be turned away so soon, after only a summer. She raised her hand and he was there before she knocked, springing up from a chair near the door.

Without a word he closed the door behind him and walked her back to the curb, and there he told her that his wife had tried to drown herself. They had parted a year ago, they had not seen each other in that time, but she had driven up the coast to go into the waves at his doorstep. She had waited on the sand for darkness, and then she had gone beyond the farthest breakers. Out there, overcome by terror, she had struggled back to shore and knocked at his door. She was sleeping now. Early on he had told Ilona about their many partings, that each parting was his wife's decision and that it was expected of him to be always waiting for her to return. Someone, he told Ilona now, must have written to her, a friend must have told her about Ilona, he must have told her himself.

They stood at arm's length from each other, not touching, the distance between them decreed by the woman in his bed. Yet even at that distance Ilona felt the ebbing of strength from his body, as much a loss as there would have been had he gone out into the deep water and brought her back.

"Martin!"

A voice thinned by fear was calling him from the passage, and Ilona thought—You have always to be prepared for a voice like that out of the past, calling the name of the lover.

His wife found her way out from the dark passage and, leaning against the porch, looked at Ilona, the woman who had come to spend the night with him. And how did she appear to his wife? There she stood on the curb—Ilona— quite thin, wearing an old raincoat, her hair in disarray even before the wind off the ocean had got to it, and were all her attempts at beauty futile? The mascara, the necklace of blue glass beads, the high heels? There she stood, her hand over the place just above her breasts, a gesture to protect herself from the pain of not being the one, the incomparable one whom his wife must have imagined.

Without wanting to, Ilona glimpsed them as she drove away. They were going back through the passageway, his arm around her shoulders, her arm across his waist. They must have walked together in just that way to rooms where they lay down to love, and now together again they went back into his rooms that his wife must have wondered about from hundreds of miles away, rooms known to other women, unknown to her. Only the address had been known to her, which door to knock at.

Ilona had counted the days, imagining how it was in those rooms by the ocean. His wife must have knocked at his door when he was sweeping the faded rugs that kept off some of the cold of the concrete floor, or when he was spreading clean sheets on the bed, or clearing away from the table his manuscript pages and newspapers and magazines and apple cores and walnut shells, when he was shaping up his rooms for Ilona, the woman who was coming to him that night. Someone knocked at his door shyly. On his doorstep—his wife, streaming ocean water, and all expectation of pleasure for that night, for any night the rest of his life, and all desire for pleasure, was swept away. If this woman on his doorstep had drowned out there he would have grieved the rest of his life. He brought her into the room, he peeled off her wet clothes, he turned on the heater and bundled her in under all his blankets. Then he sat in a chair by the bed, wiping her face lovingly, stroking her wet hair, the cold salt clinging to his fingers, stiffening them. She must

31

have said *I got scared out there* and he must have imagined her out in the darkening ocean, lifted by the swells and swept under all night long while he lay with the woman who was receding so suddenly, so far into the past that he forgot her name.

Seven nights after the night he had turned her away, he phoned her after midnight. He had driven his wife back to San Diego, where she lived with a lover, where she was enrolled in the university. He had driven his wife's car, taking the route through the valley because she had driven up the coast route, along that precariously high and narrow road above the ocean. Then he had caught a plane back to San Francisco, unlocked his door, and called Ilona. After the last parting a year ago, his wife had written that all the capitals of the world were open to her now. She had written to him like a girl writing to a brother, and in the year apart she had confided in him just as she had done when they were together, she had told him about her lovers, she had told him her hopes for herself. But when she heard that another woman might take her place and be loved above all others, then the world with all its capitals had dwindled down to nothing.

"This time," he said, "this time we convinced each other the world is still out there. It's still out there for both of us"—his voice dimmed by the sound of the heavy waves shaking the air.

When Ilona came to him again and lay down with him

where his wife had lain, she felt the other woman's fear of abandonment, and while he slept the night seemed a night already in the past. She heard the calls and wails of the little children in the house above and the mother's bare feet across the floor, she heard the man who lived on the other side of the passageway, in rooms like Martin's, wander out and come back again, over and over, and she wondered foolishly if everyone's restlessness was brought on by the man beside her, if it seemed to them that in his basement rooms he was devising a miraculous future for himself, leaving them all behind. They probably weren't thinking about him, they weren't troubled about whether or not they were to figure in his memory. Only herself, the woman beside him, was already adrift in his past.

5

There were so many mailboxes fixed to the wall of the passageway between the sidewalk and the courtyard that her own sometimes seemed missing. It couldn't be found, first attempt. While she waited for Martin to return in his own time and from wherever he was in the world, freed at last by the work that had kept him captive, freed by the praise for that work as if those who praised wore rings of keys that opened the doors of cells, a profusion of letters and postcards arrived from Venice, from Madrid, from Amsterdam, from London, and she would climb the first flight of stairs and turn and climb the next flight, reading.

The foreign airmail stationery was of a fine, soft texture and subtle colors, and his handwriting over this weightless paper—careful but not precise, quick but still contemplative—and all the postcards of paintings in museums enabled her to imagine him among the places he described. She imagined him possessed by all there was to see, euphoric one moment and dazed the next by the realization that he was never to see it all.

One among the many postcards was Rembrandt's portrait of himself when he was a young man, and she gazed at that one for a long time. The face was partly in shadow, the small, black eyes so alive and quick in that shadow, and the rest of the face and each hair of his head radiant, lit by the ruddy gold light of a day four centuries ago or by lamplight on a winter night. The postcard came the same day as the letter from her brother, and her tactic to postpone opening the letter was to gaze for a long time at the portrait. If she gave herself over to the beauty of that face it might reflect itself on all human faces, among them her brother's face. It was a superstitious act, an attempt to redeem her brother, and she had done the same thing with a portrait of Copernicus she'd found in a book on astronomers, and that man's narrow, bony face above the ecclesiastic's collar, his sideways gaze sliding away from the painter's concentration upon him, resembled even more closely her brother's face, and she imagined Copernicus living incognito as a poor, demented soul in a rented room in Chicago just to see how different the universe could look. Sometimes she imagined that, if only her brother's face was calm, his dark eyes lucid, then it might resemble the tenderly beautiful face of the young Chekhov.

On coarse tablet paper, her brother's letter was composed in the formal style taught him by his father, who had taught him to read and to write, and the pencil was pressed down hard, key words emphasized in red pencil.

My dear sister,

In order not to beat around the bush I must confess I am afraid. There is a pain in the region of my heart and I intend to find out what it means. In the meantime, please give serious thought to my plea. I assure you I will not be a burden if you allow me to live with you. I will find a job and we can share expenses. You might also consider Chicago. You can rent a room for yourself and your child in the Nestor apartments. It is clean and comfortable here. The landlady will prepare a room for you as I have already told her about this possibility. Since you have never informed me about how you make a living I guess you are a jack of all trades. If that is the case you can rest assured you can always find a job in Chicago.

A child only half his age when he was twenty, she had been his mentor and his guide out in the streets of the city, out in the world of terrors and threats, a child keeping step with his long, erratic steps, her eyes down to hide her shame over him and her shame over that shame, an entanglement of shame, and to hide herself from the wary, fascinated, mocking faces that watched them approach and pass by— the poor young madman in dead men's clothes from salvage stores, clothes too big or too small, and his sister with the snarled hair and the soiled dress that was twisted in places because she had stitched a tear wrong. She had not seen him for almost twenty years, not since the day they parted in the empty bungalow on the edge of Los Angeles, the yellow stucco bungalow that was probably not there anymore. An apartment house was probably there, layer on layer of other families living above a memory they knew nothing about. She had kept from him the way she made a living, by ephemeral stories, a way that often, very often, seemed a cowardly evasion, a dense dreaming, a delusion of omnipotence that enabled others, who were wide awake, who knew what they were doing, to slip the floor out from under her feet. He would be unable to grasp it, she knew, because it was less substantial, less meaningful, with less of a future than the way he made *his* living, scrubbing pots and pans in hospital kitchens, mopping the floors of restaurants and museums, pushing an ice cream cart through the heat of summer, and if he *did* grasp it, then his very understanding would convince her that both of them were awry, sister and brother closely resembling each other, both so uncomprehending of the world and so willful about how it was to be imagined.

You will recall I told you about my job in the Cook County hospital. A steel splinter from a brush got into my finger and caused blood poisoning to set in and I didn't know it. Imagine that! I was visiting an elderly gentleman who has an apartment down on the first floor. He used to be a pastry cook at the Palmer House and he has a stove in his room and bakes pastries. He saw the red streak up my arm and escorted me to a doctor who gave me a shot. My friend kept me in his room and applied hot, wet cloths to my arm, day and night.

Although he was happy to be tended by a friend out in the world, wasn't it true that his sister ought to be the one tending him, just as she had protected him from what the world might do to him, the years when she had walked beside him and sat beside him on trolleys and buses, her small presence never enough to keep his fear from breaking out as a cold sweat over his face, never enough to convince him he was not at the world's mercy.

Six, seven years ago he had sent her a snapshot of himself. It might be lost, it must be lost. She found it now where she knew it was, at the bottom of a shoebox of snapshots, and, sitting on the floor of the closet, she examined once more the man in the little picture. He was afraid of the camera—

she could see that and she knew why. Who was it on any film but a ghost and who wants to see his own ghost? The one in this snapshot was a man at a picnic in a park in Chicago. You could tell by his stance he was tall and didn't know what to do with his tallness, you could see he was thin because of his fear over his body and how it might trick him and do him harm. The pantslegs of his suit were somewhat short and so were the sleeves. But a tie! White cuffs! His forehead had spread upward into the dark wavy hair to become a likeness of the noble brow, and whoever had taken the picture of this man trying to smile, this childlike eccentric, had no way of knowing who he had been in his youth and what tumult had gone on in that stucco bungalow in the weeds.

She, Ilona Lewis, who had vowed to herself to see that certain persons would not pass by unknown, even if all she could do was imagine with a few faltering words their inaccessible selves, had deliberately forsaken one and that one was her brother.

6

When she opened the door to Martin she asked herself several questions and gave herself answers, all in the space of a moment. Was he taller than before? No, he was always tall and you can't grow several inches in three months if you've reached your full height already. He weighed more? No. Or maybe yes. His face, then? Was it any different? His face was larger, even broader than before. But that was not true either. Was he changed or was he not? The enigma came right along with his familiar presence and with the tears that rise at the appearance of someone who's been away for a long time and whose absence is like a hint of forever. He was the same and yet he was changed in her eyes by the thousands of strangers who saw his face in photographs many times over, an hypnotic repetition, and who, before, had no idea he existed.

In that same moment he appeared to be asking himself why he had come here and who she was. Then he stepped inside and embraced her. He went ahead of her down the little hallway, and in the kitchen he sat down at the table, lifting the lamp to the edge as considerately as he would have moved a sleeping cat. They had spoken only each other's name, nothing else.

"Would you like wine? Would you like tea?" Was her voice lost among the countless other voices from wherever he'd been and wherever he was to go? She had dreamed of him often while he was away, and in one dream he was leaning against a doorjamb, framed by the doorway, just stopping by to tell her he was on his way elsewhere, smiling over the thought of someone who was waiting for him, unseeing of her alarm, of the grief that woke her. The figure in the dream stood between her and the man in the familiar wrinkled raincoat with the twisted belt, the man at her table, the table where they had talked the night away, so many nights, back in that house on the mountainside, the man who had seen in her face, then, a spirit deserving of benevolent curiosity, even of love, the man watching her now.

"It's me," he said. "There's nobody here but me."

Then he stood up and she came to him, and he was not the stranger at the door and not the man in the dream. Their arms around each other, they roamed up and down the hallway and in and out of rooms. They roamed the neighborhood and back without knowing they'd gone out, both of them entertained by the comic adventures of Martin Vandersen out in the real world. Strangers, he told her, strangers on the street, in theater lobbies, in restaurants, on planes, recognized his face and failed to know his name, once giving his face the name of a novelist incomparably more famous and twice his age, and once the name of a young French film star, dead years ago, and she wondered if the famous ones, each undeniably different from the rest, bore a striking resemblance one to the others, even so.

Along the windowsills were the postcards he'd sent, among them the hotel postcard from Los Angeles. On the back he'd written *That's me in the lower left corner. See what's become of me?* The little figure in the photo of guests around the swimming pool was a bald man whose belly ballooned out over his yellow swim trunks. In that vast pink stucco hotel, he told her now, he'd had a suite of his own, his own postage-stamp-size patio with palm tree, steak and lobster in the restaurants, and the use of a long white convertible, everything paid for by the producer who had bought the screen rights to his novel and for whom he was writing

42

the script. *Some rewards*, he had written on the postcard, *are for something other than what you think you've done. It's a case of mistaken identity.*

Spain, after that, and the villa on the Costa del Sol, one of the hideouts of the American director and that was no hideout at all but a mecca for notables from all over the world. A general from Israel, a Zen priest from Kyoto, an Italian novelist, a soprano from Austria, a British historian—all had been guests in the time he was there, some singly, some together. And where did he go when he was alone again?

"That will take years," he said. "I'll keep you awake all night long for a year." But he began, at random. "From Malaga to Seville the road winds up among steep, dry hills, and on the slopes are chalk-white villas, far apart, and when you approach Seville you see great piles of golden wheat and a gold haze over the fields. I went to Avila, too. The town is enclosed in ancient stone walls, immensely high, and outside I saw an old woman in black sitting on the grass, sewing, and she was so small at the foot of those walls and she was so used to them. I came back to Madrid on the evening train, and the moon, the full moon, looked like it must have looked centuries ago when people were in awe of it. So close, alive, just about to say something in a voice that would fill the sky, a marvel of a moon. The train stopped along the way at village stations, and young girls were hanging around, flirting with the civil guards, and the light inside the stations was gold because of the white moonlight outside."

Spain was like the moon to her, Europe was like the moon. She hadn't been there, and when anyone assumed she had, she underwent some confusion, some embarrassment, as if caught in a lie. Because she had sent characters of hers there, they figured she had gone there too, before the imaginary ones could even buy their tickets.

"In Madrid I spent four, five days in the Prado Museum, hours in that room where they've got Goya's paintings from that time toward the end of his life they call his Black Period. When he painted those ghoulish, goatlike creatures. Maybe he was in a black period most of his life. Look at his *Disasters of War*, the terrible things we do to one another, the atrocities, where else was he but in a black period? I looked at those paintings wishing I could be abysmally true, like him, only with words. No fooling around anymore. What I did with my novel, I think I had to make the tragic palatable, like tell a few jokes, because if you take a long look at it, it's indescribable. Maybe I'll become like Claud and never write another word."

She had imagined him wandering the museums ecstatic, the praise for his own work persuading him to give up his disparagement of himself and accept a kinship with the great ones, and now, ashamed of her mistake, she kissed

44

him, and her kiss was a way to ask forgiveness for something he didn't even know about.

It was ten o'clock at night and they were at the kitchen table again. His raincoat hung on the back of his chair and he reached around into a deep pocket and unfolded on the table a large manila envelope. Several smaller envelopes of various colors slid out—blue, lavender, coral, one decorated with sprigs of flowers. Along with the letters came clippings from newspapers and magazines, some with his picture, and the face that the host had held up high for all to see appeared once again. All this had been given him by his editor in New York, yesterday, and he had read the letters on the plane. They were from strangers, some reminding him that they had met or that they had been fast friends in grammar school or in high school or in college, in cities where he had never been. One man recalled the day they climbed the mountain together, the mountain in Montana that rose above the acres of wheat and the farmhouse where the two brothers were born, the mountain that existed only in the novel. Another man claimed to have been present at the death of the younger brother, a medic in the 1st Infantry Division in Vietnam, but Martin's brother, who had served him as the character, was alive if not well in a veterans' hospital. From out of the envelope decorated with flower drawings—a snapshot of a girl. A lovely face, dark curls, and her letter confessed her hope that someday they would meet because she had recognized him as the man she was to love above all others. Whatever, whomever they wrote about, whether about themselves or about him, all their letters were saying the same thing between the lines. *You are some-one who sees, so please see me. You are someone who is seen, so please see me.* His voice unmarred by vanity, he read them aloud, puzzled, like someone learning to read a for-eign language, and she saw that he was cured of his talent for witty ridicule; his writing outstripped that lesser talent. Some of the reviews likened his vision to that of the great novelists who wrote about peasants and farmers—Hamsun and Giono and Turgenev. She gazed at his face in the lamp-light as he read and, though his voice was disbelieving, his face was calmed by that resemblance, grateful for that shared wisdom.

When everything was back in the large envelope and back again in his raincoat pocket, he looked around the kitchen and down the hallway so narrow they had bumped their elbows against the walls the many times they'd gone back and forth, arms around each other. "It's small, isn't it?"— asking and answering.

Above them a quarrel was going on, the voices even more distinct than those upstairs in the house by the ocean. Then he told her that the couple—"What's their name? Jerome? Is that their name?"—had invited him, via a letter from Claud, to stay with them until some friends of theirs left for

46

France, and then he could sublet their friends' house indefinitely. Solitude for each was a sound reason for their living apart for a while longer, a reason Ilona supplied but only in thought, a reason to protect herself against the pain of not hearing him say *Come live with me*. She was not afraid of solitude, she had weathered it often, she desired it often, but now she wondered what there was to fear in solitude that had not been there before.

"Give me your hand."

She laid her hand on the table, palm down. From a pocket of his jacket he took a small white box, turned her hand up, and placed the box in her palm.

"Open it."

She had never felt a need for gifts from a lover, from anyone, and so she failed to know, at first, what the box meant, and only gazed down at it, waiting for him to tell her.

"Ilona. Open it."

Gold earrings in the shape of a rose, a seed pearl in each one. But when she looked up, something in his large clear eyes said to her, without his knowing, *I'll forget I gave you this*. If there was a roomful of observers, not one would see the gift as a sign of his departure. They would see it as a token of love, and it was that, too. It was both, and maybe that was why she had never wanted gifts, because they were mementos of love.

A continent and an ocean separated them when they lay

down together, and every caress was a failed attempt to bridge the distance, and though he held her as he fell asleep, wanting not to lose her while he slept, he took a sudden fall into sleep and was gone.

7

No light was on behind the bamboo screen at Claud's window, the nights she walked by. She had not seen him since that paroxysm of a party in honor of the man who wasn't there. When, at last, the light was on in his room she could not bring herself to knock. She went on down the hill toward the piers, wishing that his window was dark, and contradicting that wish with another—that he would open the door just as she was passing by again and invite her in and tell her, without her asking, about Martin.

While Martin was still a guest in the couple's house he had come by often to be with her through the night, and in her few small rooms he had seemed to be wandering in a vast space. At night the red and white quilt that had belonged to his grandfather lay over them. He had loved his grandfather dearly, and his leaving the quilt with her seemed a promise that someday they would live together again. The nights she lay alone the quilt over her was like intimate knowledge of him as a child, like proof of kinship, but when he lay beside her whatever she had imagined about his childhood became an intrusion on his life in the present. He was absent though he was there. One night, while he sat on the bed taking off his shoes, he looked down at the quilt wonder-ingly, as if he had never seen it before. She was already under the quilt, and from the corner of his eye he saw her watching him and gazed back at her, and recognition dark-ened his eyes. But when he lay down beside her, his caresses were as unseeing of her as they had been since his return. The last time she heard from him was a few days after he had moved into the house of the couple who had gone to France. He had phoned to tell her where he was, and that was all. After three weeks of silence, a silence she kept be-cause she was afraid to hear again the stranger's voice, she had phoned because of fear over him. If, before his recog-nition, he had seemed destined to become a venerable old man, in the silent weeks she became deeply mindful of how visible he was now and how vulnerable. It was a reversal of her illusion that if you were recognized for your wisdom, for your art, for whatever was admirable, you became invulnerable, you might even live forever. She had phoned him at last and got no answer, and that was yesterday.

Once more she came by Claud's window on her way up from the piers. Fine as broomstraw, the bamboo screen was made almost transparent by the light in the room. Claud was sitting on the floor, reading. She saw the many books in their orange-crate bookcases and remembered something he'd told Martin—that every time he found a book by one of his own beloved writers in somebody else's house he felt a pang of jealousy, like a boy whose parents are showing love toward another child, a complete stranger.

A flicker of embarrassment in his eyes when he saw who it was at his door—a woman who had come to hear something she didn't want to hear. With one arm he gestured toward the lumpy armchair, with the other he offered the bed, and the entire small room was made available to whatever her response was to be when he told her what he knew. Anyone who leads you further into the way things are appears to be an enemy, but, watching him close the curtains, she felt an impulse of gratitude, a crucial last-minute impulse to make a comrade of him before he became an enemy.

"She left her husband," he said.

Then, "Sit down."

She was afraid to move. If she moved she'd fall away from her lodging in Martin's life.

51

Sparing her his sight of her, he turned his back. "She bought a house over on the mountain, up beyond where you used to live. All you've got to remember is. . . ." He must be groping for some truism that would take care of everything. "She hasn't invited me over so I've never been there myself, but he's pointed it out to me from this side of the bay, more or less where it is. A little closer to heaven."

In the past, when this man had seemed not to see her, he must have known about this moment and avoided the sight of her, even then.

"Sit down, Ilona."

Some closeted figure within her was warning her that if she sat down it would reveal itself, its fragile, cloistered self that was unprepared for assaults common to all. Out in the world there was a terrible prevalence of assaults that put to shame this one.

"All you need to remember," he said, "is that your imagination finds more bliss for them than they find for themselves."

A trembling took her over, and she turned toward the door, wanting to run out. Instead, she stayed where she was, to hear more. He was wrong, this man. He had figured it out in reverse. The bliss of lovers was the reality and your imagination came nowhere near. When she turned back toward him he was sitting on the edge of the bed, watching her, and she saw at once, with surprisingly sharp sympathy, how his face contrasted with that of his friend Martin, whose face always expected great tidings, as if a promise had been made to him at birth. The promise was missing from this man's face, or it had passed before his eyes on its way somewhere else.

"Women with that gaze, you never forget them," he said. "Those melancholy beauties. They look at a man that way and he thinks he's the one she's been waiting for. I used to think it was me she had her eyes on. I imagine Anna Karenina looked that way, and Emma Bovary. Maybe Frieda looked at D. H. that way when he came to visit her husband. Women like that are always waiting for the lover to show up and they don't have to wait long, they just wait over and over. Oh yes, and Helen. Sailed away with Paris, the guest who came to stay just a few days. You've read Seferis? For me the greatest poet alive. So many of his lines—it's like we used to say in school—I know them by heart. She wasn't really there at Troy, but nobody knew that, 'and Paris, Paris lay with a shadow as though it were a solid form, and we slaughtered ourselves for Helen ten long years, and the rivers swelled, the blood bedded in muck, all for a linen undulation, a bit of cloud, a butterfly's flicker, a swan's down, an empty tunic, all for a Helen.' I like the idea she wasn't there, it helps me when a woman looks right through me as if I'm air. I think—You're not there either, baby, you cause trouble but you're not who everybody thinks you are, you're a figment of our dumb imagination. Martin told me it got so strong between them he had to leave. I don't know how long he intended to stay. Maybe he set his suitcase down on that blue rug of theirs and thought he was on the Aegean Sea forever. He moved into a hotel until he could move into that place he's in now. She used to come to the hotel."

Lovers obliterate you. She imagined them in the husband's presence, unable even to glance at each other because a glance would reveal to him how far from them he was, swept way back into the past, and when Martin came to be with her, those nights when he was living with the couple, he had set a vast space around the lovers and she was nowhere. A necessary cruelty the lovers mistook for kindness. *Oh let's not hurt him, oh let's not hurt her. Let's simply make them disappear.*

She began to button her coat and realized she hadn't unbuttoned it. He was wrong again, this man. It wasn't melancholy in the eyes of those women, it was serenity, it was like that sweet stun in the eyes of children who've been given a gift they never asked for, a gift too much to ask for.

Lamed by grief she climbed the hill and when she reached her street she turned, and there it was across the bay, across the black waters—the glittering mountain—and facing that spectacle of lights was like facing the lovers, their unseeing eyes.

# 8

At four in the morning she was kneeling on the floor of the dark kitchen, dialing his number. She had taken the phone down from the table because this trespass had to be done in a crouch, so she could not be seen, so she could protect her breast from his voice, from his presence on the other side of the city or from his absence, over there. She expected him not to be home. He was with the woman in the woman's house. They were lying together in that depthless sleep of separation after loving, that falling away from the wondrous balancing of one by the other. Or they were in his bed, in that house where she had never been, and the ring of the phone was waking them both. If he answered, what would she ask of him? Something beyond the possible? That he become himself again, change back into himself?

"I'm afraid."

"Of what?" He must be standing nude, he always slept nude. Or on his way to the phone he might have wrapped himself in a robe, he might own one now. Neither had a robe when they were together. Robes belonged to the infirm or to those who preferred sleeping to waking. But the woman might have given him an elegant robe that made him even more precious to the giver.

"Ilona? What are you afraid of?"

Every night she slept for an hour or less and was waked by the pounding of her heart. Her heart had become a tyrant, leaping up in fear of itself.

"Of what? Of what?"

"I'm a good person." It made no sense.

"I know you're a good person."

"I'm dear to some. I'm dear to my child."

"Yes you are."

There was no way to ask him to be her comrade again if only for a few minutes, only long enough to assure her that she was not someone who deserved to be left, not untouchable, not like the millions of untouchables, way over on the

56

other side of the world and too many centuries old to even think about.

"Ilona?"

"Can I come over? When it's daylight, I mean?" Never had she begged for anything from anybody. Unless, without knowing it, she had begged the very air, all her life.

"So early?"

"I mean in the morning. I need to tell you something." She didn't know yet, herself, what it was she had to tell him.

He was waiting.

"I mean when I come. I need to tell you something when I come."

He said nothing, reluctantly waiting for that something to be laid upon him.

"Please tell me how to get there."

When it was over she bent her head to the floor, covering her eyes to hide herself away from the woman's sight of her, from her sight of the woman lying in his bed, her body covered with that shimmer of bliss that had covered her own in the past.

・・・・・・・・・・・ CHAPTER ・・・・・・・・・・

# 9

The long view of Market Street on a Sunday morning, the trolleys few and far between and only two and three persons in sight, moving slowly through the heat of yesterday and of the day to come and through pale sunlight not yet reflected on glass and metal, an odd light like that of the first minutes of an eclipse. Waiting on the corner for a trolley that would take her into his neighborhood, she was again a trespasser into other people's lives, someone who insists upon saying something about the self regardless of the hour.

The clanging trolley carrying her along was like her own ridiculous will. Unassuming persons should always be suspect. Sooner or later, when the time comes, their will takes over, their unanswerable desires take over. She kept her head bent with the shame of this tumult over the end of love. It happened to almost everybody, it was as widespread as other misfortunes, but it was the one to keep quiet about.

When she stepped down from the trolley it was just as he had described it to her—she was facing west, facing a steep hill, and just as expected her heart was terrified, a tyrant terrified of itself. The climb up the hill was as tiring as it would be if the day were already over. At the top of the hill, on a corner, there it was—a gray frame house, small among the houses and apartments that covered the hill.

Where was the front door? There, at the end of an archway of dusty, flowering shrubbery, and she imagined the woman passing along under this arbor, coming and going, the woman loved above all others, the incomparable one.

"I won't stay long." Not long, only long enough to plunge them into everything unanswerable from where it took forever to rise.

He kissed her on the lips, perhaps to placate her, perhaps to pretend he was glad to see her, unseeing of how his kiss deprived her of him.

Off in a kitchen he fixed tea while she stayed in the living room by a window, afraid to turn toward the room, immobilized by the presence of the woman for whom the house

59

and all its objects were familiar. The woman was the atmosphere of the house. She wondered if she had forgotten to comb her hair or wash her face. Was there some gray in her hair she'd discover when she got home? If you bow your head for so many years over your endless unknowing, over your imagination that substitutes for knowing, then how surprised you are, when you lift your head, to find yourself older than when you began.

The interior of this house was to puzzle her memory for years. It was a small house but like a maze where experiments are carried on with captive creatures—a reward somewhere, you had only to find it. She was never to get the scheme of it straight, where one room belonged in relation to another. She was to remember only that she roved through the house, never recognizing a room where she'd been before no matter how many times that day.

Each waited for the other's first words, one mind in fear of the other, and the moment she sat down to accept a cup the unspeakable self spoke up. "I can't be like her."

"Why do you say that?"

Then she was up and roving, leaving untouched the teacup that the woman drank from. "I can't be like her, I can't be serene like her. You told me I was troubled in my soul, you made me feel like I had something you didn't want to catch, but most of the time I was calm, most of the time we were comrades, most of the time we felt love. If there's trouble in me, and there is trouble, it's the nameless kind that's all right to feel because I'm human and I feel, and it's not just over me, it's over so much more than me."

Her voice was loud and harsh, a voice not her own and yet her own but never heard before. So many times, people had to bend their heads to hear her, afraid they'd been stricken deaf. Then she heard that voice say something she herself would never say. "Oh I wish I were her!"

It was shameful, it should never be said and never even thought—the wish to be somebody else. The wish to be that other woman was a betrayal of everyone in her life whose life seemed entrusted to her for safekeeping, even if only in memory, a betrayal of everyone whose life was more precious to her than her own. The wish to be that other, any other, was to set them all adrift.

In a corner now, cornered by her own self, she was saying something she couldn't believe she was saying, so archaic, so demented, so lost was its meaning. "You're among the blessed ones now, you know."

Nobody thought that way anymore, and she waited for his denial that would relieve her of the idea, relieve him and herself of the burden of it. She waited for a small, scoffing, uncomfortable laugh, at least.

A wind, stirred up by the heat of the days and nights, swept the curtains out over the sills, and a door in another house slammed shut, a distant sound warning of listeners. That voice of hers saying crazy things could be heard by whoever was in the apartment house across the street, by whoever was passing along the sidewalk. He shut the windows and pulled down the white blinds, and went into other rooms to do the same.

A white glare filled the room now, and she was to remember herself roving through that glare in the heat of the day, trapped by her own self within that house she was never to enter again, within rooms that would puzzle her memory like a maze.

When he came back into the room where she waited in her corner, he had an answer for her. "Maybe I am among the blessed."

At the front door she had seen at a glance that his face was mute, a mask concealing his life from her, and she had avoided glancing at him again. But now she looked to see if he were agreeing with her only because he hadn't heard it right. She had wanted him not to agree with her. Nobody was blessed and nobody abandoned. The world wasn't like that.

"Maybe I belong where I was before."

Where was that? Was it where he had thought he was when he was with her? Was it among all those in the dark?

Though the room was between them, he was too near. A door was open to another room and she went in. A bed covered with a sea-blue spread. A bureau with two silver candlesticks, the white candles burned low. On a chair a woman's silk kimono, pale green and amber and garnet, mingling in exquisite harmony, the woman's own colors.

Tonight he would recover from this day. She left the room the moment she entered it.

In the doorway she was caught by him and embraced, and in his body against hers she felt that same ebbing away of his strength, that same bafflement over a woman's coercive need of him just as on that night his wife had gone into the waves at his doorstep, and she longed to embrace him and protect him from herself, the enigma that was herself.

"Sit down with me," he begged.

She went with him to the couch but she would not sit down with him. An unbending will had taken possession of her body. She stood above him, and he drew her between his knees and bowed his head against her. Someone years ago had seen in her some goodness of heart, even some beauty of spirit, and only now was she remembering. Was it this man? And had he told her not in words so much as in his embrace of her?

"My heart wakes me all night long," she told him.

"My heart wakes me too."

She hadn't expected that.

"Nobody but you makes me cry," he said.

What did he mean? If she had come to be told that, yes, she was a good person, yes, comprehending of the lovers despite the trouble she was giving them, if she had come to be told this, was he telling her that her striving to be wise was enough to make him weep, so futile was that striving?

She broke away. Flowering plants, ferns in humid air—a

conservatory? No, it was only a small room next to the kitchen. A bare table, a mug of cold coffee, a few crumbs. The windowpanes were rattling in the warm wind and a fly was crawling along the sills and tapping against the hot glass. It was really a modest kind of house. But when the woman sat here at this table, the flow of morning sun, patterned with the shadows of leaves, must appear like a lovely scarf floating around her, and he would paint her as Bonnard would have painted her, her hair ablaze with sun and summer fruit on the table. Back in his rooms by the ocean the walls had glowed with museum prints—portraits of women who had mesmerized the artists years ago, centuries ago, and when he had lain asleep beside her those women had seemed to be the women in his dreams or all icons of one woman.

A door led to the backyard, and Martin stepped out into the wind and the sun. She watched him through the window as he knelt to set a plant upright. One sundown, out on the cold stretch of beach, they had come upon a shore bird whose wings were covered with oil. A few days before, fuel oil spilled from a tanker and hundreds of birds were dying. He had knelt and clasped the bird in his strong, gentle hands though it pecked at his hands with its long sharp beak, and they had taken it to a bird refuge to be cleansed. Watching him kneeling now to attend to a living thing, she saw how he could be mesmerized by a woman's desire for more of life, for him, and by his own desire for more life.

The boughs of a tree in the next yard hung over the high

fence between the yards, and she sat down in their shadows that were swept back and forth across the grass. She was always surprised by gardens in the city. This one was a tangle of dry grass, tomato plants, and geraniums. From over the fence drifted the sweet, lulling music of glass wind-chimes hanging from a branch. Years back, in her neighborhood of bungalows on the edge of Los Angeles, glass windchimes hung on the front porch of a bungalow where something violent had gone on, the nature of it kept from her, a child. The bungalow was empty, no one lived there after that, but the windchimes went on tinkling, stirred by the slightest breeze.

Martin sat down beside her in the confusion of sun and shade, and stroked her hands. "Your hands are beautiful." They were not, the knuckles and fanlike bones too visible. Some caresses of hers that had conveyed to him her sight of beauty in his own being—he might mean *that*.

"Who are the ones you say are blessed?"—his voice carried away by the wind and back again.

"I just *suppose* they are"—her voice her own again. "You have to see that my mind isn't altogether gone."

"Who do you *suppose* they are?"

She lay down on the coarse, dry grass. "Nobody is."

But something comic about his request for simple answers freed her to consider who they might be. Once again she let herself believe that simple answers were always hovering around and she had only to catch one on the wing.

"Explorers, I guess. Where nobody's been before, each

one in his chosen territory. Even though they go so high or
so deep they can't breathe anymore. They might be."

She didn't know what she was talking about and she
didn't want to look up and see his listening face. She could
see only his shirt and how the shadows and sun moved
across it in quick succession.

"Go on."

"I guess great singers." They would do as well as any.

"Could you speak a little louder?"

"I said great singers."

"I heard that so far."

"Say a great soprano, and the audience stands up and
applauds for a long time, and you're standing up with the
rest and as the applause goes on and on you notice you've
got tears in your eyes. Say you're up in the balcony and you
can see the rest of the audience below and you can see the
little figure on the stage, and her head is bowed."

No answer, no comment. He must be giving it serious
thought.

"Or say a great composer. What if you'd heard Beethoven
play the piano, his own music? A friend of his said that his
bearing was masterfully quiet, noble, and beautiful. You'd
feel you were in the presence of someone blessed, wouldn't
you?"

"I hear," he said.

"But if he was blessed he didn't know it. In one of his bad
times he wrote to a friend 'A man may not voluntarily part

with his life so long as a good deed remains for him to per-
form.' Maybe he didn't know his good deed was his music.
Or maybe he knew it but not all the time."

She glanced up to see him nod because she knew he
wasn't going to do more than nod.

After a while, "Who else?"

Who else? Who else? The number had to be small.

"I missed that one."

"No, I said nothing." Lost as it was out there in the wind,
her voice wanted to retreat still farther to its usual refuge
that was silence.

"Maybe those desert fathers. They stayed in their caves,
they starved themselves. When one of them was given a gift
of sweet grapes, he passed it on. It went all around and came
back to the giver, not one grape missing. They wanted nothing, they wanted nobody around but God. Maybe they
were blessed. Or maybe they just wanted to be. I don't know.
I never tried to name any before."

"Go on anyway."

Go on anyway. "Would you say those persons who give
their lives for others? The ones who spend their whole lives
that way because it *is* their life. Even though they die for
others, even though they're executed or assassinated.
Would you say they are?"

No answer. Only a waiting silence.

"A while ago I was looking at a book about the Spanish
architect, Antonio Gaudi. Could he be one?"

Almost impatiently, "How do I know?"

"Everybody loved him. The whole country. He was like a saintly child, he was so deeply religious. One evening he was on his way home from the cathedral he'd designed and he was struck down by a trolley car and he lay there in the street, an old man in old clothes, and nobody knew who he was, and no taxi driver would take him to the hospital. They thought he was just a derelict. Somebody got him to a hospital and he was put in the paupers' ward, where he died. By then friends had gone in search of him and then everybody knew who he was, this poor old man with snow white hair, and cries of sorrow went up all over Spain."

"Anybody else?"

"Astronomers?"

"You're the one who's picking."

"Astronomers, I guess. Like Galileo, like Copernicus. Can you imagine how they felt? Their heads filled with those great aerial charts? The planets spinning around the sun in there? When you see their portraits all you see is their faces, but when you think about what was going on inside their heads, they must have felt blessed, don't you think so?"

The rough grass against her face was suddenly unbearable. "I remember something Michelangelo said about human beauty, how it seemed to him that God revealed his beauty that way and so it's an outward sign of spiritual beauty. No matter that I know for sure it's not so, it seems so. It seems true because it's so simple and because Michelangelo said it. But isn't it a terrible blindness to everyone else in the world?"

She sat up. "No, I can't anymore. I don't know who is or who isn't. It's a waste."

"No great writers? The long dead ones?"

"They could be."

"They wouldn't agree."

"No, I guess they wouldn't. I remember an old German book of pictures of the death masks of great artists and composers and writers from all over Europe, and the faces of the composers and the sculptors seemed serene, as if they were on their way to paradise, but the faces of the writers were tormented."

She brought her knees up and bent her head to them, closing her eyes, wanting not to see him. It was absurd, this pursuit of something always elusive—an answer to why there was so much light around the few, even centuries after they were last seen on earth, and why the rest went down in the dark.

"Ilona?"

"I hear you."

"Do *you* think they were?"

"Maybe everybody thought they were just because they tried to rescue people—us, everybody—from oblivion. Maybe the rescue was an ordeal for them because they knew in their hearts it wouldn't work after all. I remember about Chekhov, his long, long journey across Russia and Siberia to that island, Sakhalin, where the czars sent convicts. He was tubercular, he was already coughing blood, but he made that journey—floods, awful rains, cold—to record what went on there, who they were. He wrote that the street noise there was the clanking of leg irons."

Silence. Then, "No more?"

At last, and against the most resistance. "Lovers. In the beginning."

"Ilona, where do you come from?"

He began to stroke her hair consolingly as if she were a lunatic quieted down, and she wished she had kept her cumbrous delusion from this man who no longer cared to hear even the lighter ones.

# 10

The blinds changed from sunstruck white to mauve to gray. A streetlamp on the corner came on and the blinds changed to silver. In those hours the woman he loved now, the woman who resembled those portraits on the walls of night, back in his basement rooms by the ocean, seemed to be wandering the street, away and near again, and some moments so far away she might be lost out there forever. The kimono had been put away, he had slipped it away without her seeing how. Instead of a lessening of desire for him because she had become less, she felt desire as intense as in the beginning of their time together, a desire that was like the desire for life that flares up and takes possession in moments of danger.

They slept, and when she woke she was certain it was late, almost midnight. Seven, by the clock on the bureau. Martin was awake, lying on his back, very still.

"Does it seem she's always known you?" It was a question she ought to have left behind in sleep, where she must have heard it clearly spoken.

"I don't know what you mean."

Neither did she. Unless she meant that the woman he loved now must seem to him to have known him back in the years of his obscurity, when no one else had known he was already the man he was to become, when only he had known.

"She loves me, that's all I know," he said, and the longing in his voice confirmed his love for the other. "She would have loved me when I was a nobody, if that's what you want me to doubt."

She got up and with her back to him began to dress, wanting to destroy the tormentor in herself, who tormented him and herself, wanting to give in to the way things were in the world, wanting to regain an innocence from years ago, that receptive innocence to which everything offered itself.

She heard him get up and begin to dress. Somewhere in the house a phone rang. Over in her aerie the woman must be wondering why he hadn't appeared, suspecting he was caught in the maelstrom stirred up by the woman left. He closed the door to the small room where Ilona had seen a desk and books, and she heard no words, only the resonance of his voice against the door. She imagined the compulsion of love that brought the woman to phone him. More than compulsion—the conviction that she was loved and her voice always welcomed and waited for, and Ilona imagined his pleasure, his relief, hearing the voice that rescued him from his tormentor, if only for a brief moment.

When he came back she begged him, "Don't tell her what I'm feeling. Never tell her."

"She's compassionate," he said.

Struck a blow to her very center, she curled in on herself. Compassion from the woman he loved for the woman left— what an unbearable offering! Why didn't he know this? It was the simplest thing in the world to know. She tried to get past him in the doorway. She was dressed and she tried to get past him and go out into the world and leave him forever.

"Wait, wait, wait, Ilona."

With both fists she struck him on the chest. He caught her wrists and she struggled to be free, twisting her arms, trying to bite his hands. The woman must be watching from over there in her aerie, that serene, that knowing face watching her, the woman left, whose compassion was only a tenuous little virtue, who had none at all for these lovers. It was as if he had taken it away from her, Ilona, and given it to the other, who had already so many virtues to be loved for.

"Wait, Ilona, wait. I don't know where I am."

It calmed her a bit, his confession. If he didn't know where he was, then neither did the woman know for sure and neither did she.

Then they were wandering together through unlit rooms, arms around each other, locked in silence. After a time he began to switch on lamps, and after a time she sat down at the table in the room with the flowering plants and he began to prepare supper for them and, watching him moving about in the kitchen light, she saw him as the ultimate stranger, someone proving to her how little she knew about anyone, almost nothing about the feel of his life to him, about the desperation of his desires, and she saw herself, the woman watching him in this house that was his alone, as a censor of his life, substituting herself for life's deepenings.

Martin set plates and silver on the table, sat down across from her and served her.

"Give me your hand"—placing his left hand over her left hand, and they held their forks in their right hands but could not eat.

"I expected you to understand"—touching the tines of his fork to his brow and then to his heart. "Like you feel for your characters."

She shook her head. She understood nothing, and the

time was coming—it might already be here—when she wouldn't be able even to pretend in her work to be on the trail of even the slightest clue.

"Ilona, look at me."

No matter how gently he asked she couldn't lift her eyes. Her eyes would be so unseeing he'd wish he had never asked her to meet his eyes.

He kept his hand over hers all through the silent meal, and when they sat on the backporch steps, under faint stars and in the warm wind, he stroked her hand and stroked her hair. Voices and music from the apartments and houses around them were carried toward them and away, and the thrashing of branches was louder in the darkness.

When they lay down together to sleep he kissed her on her forehead and on her lips, lay back, clasped her hand in his hands on his chest and, breathing very quietly, fell asleep, yielding to sleep so it might bear him away. She remembered dreams he had told her about—daring escapes, false accusations that might be true, of being trapped again in the army and running amok, and she remembered a dream about her. He had sat up in sleep and called her name, though she was lying right there beside him, because he was dreaming that she was running down some stairs, away from him forever. She slept and was wakened by the certainty that this night was the last night she would sleep beside him and that no one would question him about her

75

disappearance. No one, because he was absolved of any act, any confounding of himself and others, he was absolved because his life was just as it ought to be. All the strangers out in the world who saw his work as an absolving of them for being so human, all were absolving him. It was a ridiculous idea, it was Claud's idea, it was an idea that could be thought only when Martin was asleep or when he was to be a great distance away.

The streetlamp was about to dim out, giving way to dawn. She picked up her clothes to carry them into another room so the rustling as she dressed wouldn't wake him. He was sleeping on his back again, his face upward, and she found no grateful acceptance in his face of that absolving she was granting him. A troubling lay over his face, but lightly, as if whatever was going on in the depths of sleep had a long way to rise to the surface.

A dense fog covered the city, concealing the hills below this one. Only a few patches of neighborhoods could be seen, floating islets, appearing and vanishing, in a gray sea. She went down the hill trying not to shiver. Yesterday she had come here in just a skirt and blouse, believing the hot spell was to go on forever or disbelieving she was to stay the night.

# 11

When her heart waked her in the night she would get up, slip a sweater over her pajamas, sit down at her table, and call up from the past the one who was pleading with her to rescue him, the one she had kept at a distance so that he could never be recognized as her brother. In the middle of the night, every night, she was called out on a rescue mission, fearful over whom she must rescue, not her brother alone but herself along with him. Nobody else in the world was going to get up from beside a woman passionately loved and sit down at a notebook to rescue them from the dark.

Early on in their time together, Martin had told her about himself and his farm family in Montana in an amused, indulgent way like a father of himself, and that was the way he had told about them in his novel, and when he had asked Ilona about herself she had told him a few things, hesitantly, and then more, and everything she told him seemed to have been waiting to be told just to him. It was only the usual way lovers exchange stories about their lives, hoping, without knowing they were hoping, that years later when they had lost touch with each other, what little each had learned about the other would be remembered wisely. Once when they were strolling and she glimpsed his reflection in a mirror in a store window she mistook his face for her own. They didn't resemble each other. His face was broad and the width between the eyes and their large gaze gave him the look of someone from a previous century, unknowing of the self, but his face had become the face entrusted with what she had told him about herself, so it had been easy enough to mistake his face for her own. But now this scribbling away in a dimestore notebook set her among those nocturnal souls who fill their pages—every inch and the margins too—with eternal concerns of no concern at all to anyone else. It was intended for her eyes alone and that was enough, and it was probably enough for all those others who redeem themselves and whomever they're called to redeem while everyone else sleeps on.

Over and over in memory she approached the yellow stucco bungalow in the weeds, afraid to go in and see again the ones unutterably dear, those she could not tell about because to attempt to tell was like an invasion of sacred ground, because something was protecting them from her, from fallacy, from artifice, from failure. But at last she went in, choosing—among all the weathers in which she had approached that bungalow and gone in—a summer twilight, because the sky of that time of day had been filled with promise and the deeper the blue became the more certain she had become of the existence of the world's great cities and far outposts.

She had always come home alone. She had a lover in that time, that last year, but she never brought him home to see her mother fading away in the tiny bedroom where the plaster had fallen in patches and the slats showed through like the bones of the house, and to see her brother in other men's discarded clothes, too small or too large, and to see his excited face and to hear his hollowy voice, like the voice of a desert prophet. Every stranger was the wisest being on earth for him, even the welfare worker who came at intervals since their father died to assure herself they were in need and whose eyes swelled with fear of him, the towering man leaning over her, asking her questions about persons

79

in the newspapers and in history, because wasn't it her job to collect data on everyone in the world? If Ilona were to bring a lover home, just for that lover to see who were the ones she was close to, he would have to be someone like Rilke who saw the blindman, the leper, the lunatic, with infinite compassion and whose poetry she read in the back room of the bookstore when there were no customers to wait on and no books to wrap.

Out of high school, seventeen, she had inquired at every bookstore for a job, the secondhand ones, the antiquarian ones, the ones that sold only the latest, because to work in the midst of thousands of books, no matter how cluttered, how musty, how concrete-cold the store might be, was to feel cloistered and concealed from the world and yet in the world. From the edge of the city she had ventured far into its illusory center, into a glamour core, an enclave, where she passed celebrities on the street and persons who desired nothing more devoutly than to be mistaken for celebrities, all of them confusing her eyes and widening her sight. She was hired because her stuttery shyness must have stirred the proprietor's benevolence or because she answered in an unpredictable way his predictable questions.

"Who's your favorite writer?"

"Conrad." Was that a mistake?

"Why him?"

"Because," trying to make a joke that would soften her

stiff lips, "because if God could write He'd write like Conrad."

"You mean God took a nom de plume? If He's up to tricks like that, He wouldn't be satisfied with one. Name some more."

Whenever celebrities wandered into the store, figures one hundred times smaller than they were on the screen, then something—pride or a faltering conviction of incomparably more value in the dusted books—protected her against their bedazzling selves. She would look away, and if she had to wait on them she would pretend ignorance of who they were. But sometimes they would see her hands tremble, and sometimes she lost her voice.

From the illusory capital that mesmerized the rest of the world, she rode a long way back each night to the bungalow with the stains under the windows from rain on the rusted screens and, stepping from the streetcar, she saw the racing forms, pink, green, yellow, caught in the dry weeds of the yard, tossed there by the throngs on their way back from the racetrack a mile away, the papers thrown away yesterday bleached by this day's sun. The crowds were already gone, inward bound to the city, except for a few stragglers on foot, except for some elegant cars still coming from the track, bound back to where the faultless beauties lived and those who loved them. In one—three persons: the bareheaded man at the wheel, another man on the far side, and, between the men, a lovely woman. No one in the car glanced at her, no one in the car suspected her of wondering how it felt to be so highly visible for beauty and how it felt to bring that beauty like a gift to lovers. If that face in the center were to glance out, the girl on the sidewalk might be extinguished by the secret, ideal life in the depths of that glance and by the way the eyes would slide away as if they'd seen nobody out there.

Night in that little house low to the ground, the last night, and Ilona awake in the bed that had been both hers and her mother's, and her brother calling to her from his bedroom across the hall that was not really a hall but only a cubicle of space, his voice startling her from sorrow like a cradling sleep. It was a few nights after their mother's strong will to live had left her body, taking all traces of grace and beauty meant to charm death into giving up its own inexorable will.

"Ilo?"

"Yes?"

"Ilo, let me come with you."

"Let me find out first."

"You need a man to protect you."

"Nobody's going to hurt me."

She was already twenty but for him she was the child who had protected him from terrible possibilities waiting for him everywhere, inside the city, out in vast space, and in the narrow confines of buses and streetcars, and now if she would only allow him to repay that kindness he would be grateful for the rest of his life. In the tentative silence she sensed the imploring going on in his shallow sleep where he must be offering up incontestable reasons, down on his knees. The tempest that possessed him when she was a little girl spent itself when their father died, though the furrows in his brow got deeper, and the sweat in his hair and the agitated walk and the fear in his eyes remained.

"Ilo?"

Near dawn, and he was in the doorway, a tall wraith in faded, shrunken pajamas, closely resembling an asylum inmate in an old etching she had come upon in the bookstore, and the likeness was an anointing of him, as if across a century the artist rescued him from his solitary, forsaken condition. At seven he had almost been forsaken by life, consumed by fever for days, and after that he was not who he had been, not anymore the little boy who drew intricate pictures of trains and passengers, someone in each window unlike anyone else in all the other windows.

"Ilo, we won't see each other again."

"Don't think that way."

Then from his lonely throat dry sobs rose. A few only, because he must be afraid they would turn her against him since he was not the most reliable of protectors. Like an admonition his very loneliness closed up his throat, and he went back to bed.

They sat at the table trying to eat their breakfast of dry toast. The table—where their father had taught him to read and to write, where their father, the times he was home, ate his supper in a slow, reflective way like a man far from home, where she, Ilona, had scratched away at her stories, each story a refuge into which she escaped and where no one recognized her—was to be taken away with the rest of the furniture by the mailman, with whom he had made friends and who was to pay him a few dollars.

"Ilo, you won't have to work. I'll find a job and take care of you."

It was like an offer to lame her for life, an offer to imprison her within his own benighted being forever.

"Wherever I go," she said, "let me get settled first." And this denial to him of the future he was begging from her was a cruelty that was to strike back at her when she was to sit at all the many tables of her life, roaming her imagination with the hope of finding her own future there. No latent beauty was to be revealed in her work, only the cruelty of forsaking him that confessed itself in the emptiness of each story.

"I'll go to Aunt Sarah's, I'll go to Seattle and live with her." He was striding around the room in a frenzy of helplessness. "If she can't take me in I'll get a room near her and I'll help her, I'll do her shopping for her and I'll go with her on the streetcar if she's afraid of going out alone and I'll mop the floors for her."

The old woman who was their father's sister had come down to console them when their father died and to pay for the funeral, and she had tucked her purse under her pillow at night, afraid the two demented children might steal from her while she slept.

"Then I'll know where to reach you," she said, "when the time comes for you to be with me."

He thanked her profusely for that. "If you don't do well where you go," he said, "you can come and live with me."

"If I don't do well," she promised.

Eagerly, on the run, he helped the mailman's two sons carry the furniture out to the open truck. He hoisted up his father's ancient black suitcase of heavy, pebbled leather, with straps and buckles. Up it went and over. Their father was gone most of the time, on the road, searching for work on newspapers in other cities, soliciting ads. He was on the edge of oldness when she was born, and the Sundays he took her to hear the soapbox orators in Pershing Square, people would ask him if she were his grandchild. So his suitcase was old-fashioned even then. On the run, her brother carried out grocery boxes filled with salvage store clothes, with paraphernalia of inestimable value, each box tied with twine, and, last, the wooden box with handle, containing his shoemaker's tools.

They were alone in the empty house. The mailman's sons waited, one in the driver's seat, the other on a chair in the truckbed. The seat beside the driver was to be his, like a seat of honor. He wore a black suit that some larger man, years ago, must have worn to his own significant events. He was to spend the night, or even a few nights, at the mailman's house, and she was to board a bus to San Francisco, where she had never been. It was time to part. When he bent his head to kiss her on the cheek, his loneliness struck him across the face and left him pale and shaken. He was already lost in the world he was to enter as soon as this embrace was over. He would never again be even halfway sure she loved him, though she kissed his trembling cheek and his brow filmed with sweat.

Then he climbed up into the truck and, wearing a departed man's dapper Panama hat and hunched over in fear of this exciting time, he waved to her, an exaggerated wild waving, as they drove off.

Ilona, alone at her table, raised her head and saw that it was a dark four o'clock. If it was six o'clock in Chicago, was he already on his way to his job through cold half-dark streets or was he on his way home from a hospital's steamy basement kitchen after scrubbing pots and pans all night, a tall figure, head sunk forward, hat pulled down over his ears, overcoat flapping in the wind? Or was he still asleep in that city closer than this one to the hour of waking, and if he was still asleep, his sleep was not deeper than hers had been all her waking life.

# 12

Uncertain about which door was the right one, someone was bungling along the landing, knocking at all of them. The dog inside the apartment next to Ilona's clawed at the door, banging against it, and its bellowing bark caused the walls of her room to vibrate. Then the caller knocked at her door.

"Ah, it's you," Claud said, surprised he had found her. "I want you to join me in an act of supreme cruelty. You remember Jerome, our host? If not his name at least his suffering face? We're going out to the ocean and we're going to make a bonfire and we're going to burn his manuscript. His only one, that one about his wife and Neely in the coils of a boa constrictor passion."

One second of perverse pleasure—it sprang so fast to her eyes she had no way of concealing it from him. If all those pages, all those years of labor were to go up in smoke, then the woman herself might end up unremembered, her life unknown.

"That's an awful thing to do," she said, "burning up all that labor," her dismay as true as that shameful pleasure a moment ago.

"It's cold out there at the ocean," he warned. "Dress warm."

"I don't want to see him."

She wanted to back away, close the door. They were two of a kind, herself and that husband. There was a shame about them both for their fear of loss and for the loss that had come about.

"Oh, but he looks great. He's skinny and he's got a haircut and he's wearing suits again, and he's got himself a big desk in the trust department at the Bank of America or Bank of the Cosmos. One little thing left to do, burn up his obsession, and he'll soar like a big pink flamingo."

He found her raincoat and held it up for her and she slipped it on. At the foot of the stairs he took out a black knit cap from his jacket pocket, a watch-cap like the one he was wearing, and drew it over her head, down to the eyebrows.

"You and me," he said. "I'm the executioner and you're the priest. Say a prayer over the ashes."

The time was midafternoon, but their host was lying asleep on Claud's bed. He sat up, hampered by the blankets over him, struggling up from the exhaustion that precedes an act of finality. Ilona would not have recognized him in a crowd. He was somebody else or more truly himself than on the night of his party. His face, that night, must have been padded with hope that everything would stay the same, the tolerable same, despite the man up in the air.

Claud pushed a chair firmly against the backs of her knees. "Sit down, sit down." And to the host, "Sit up, sit up. I'll brew something bitter."

Jerome sat on the edge of the bed, head down. "How've you been?" he asked his shoes.

"I've been fine," she said.

"Me too."

She had wanted never to see this man again. The night of the party, his prophetic fear of losing his wife to Martin had diminished her, Ilona. His confession had been direct as a statement that she, Ilona, was not one to keep a lover when that lover was to come into the presence of his beautiful wife. He diminished her further, now, by the loss of his flesh, by the grief and rage that had brought him here and entangled him in his friendly enemy's blankets. She was not loved beyond reason, as his wife was loved. She was not loved anymore within reason.

"You want to tell Ilona what you did? What he did," Claud went on, "was hide out by her house and wait for them to come out. He bought himself a Triumph because it's easily hidden under a bush, the sort of car a rodent can drive. He told himself he wasn't going to hurt anybody, he just wanted to see them together. Maybe he hoped the sight of them would bring on a heart attack and he'd collapse and die, like those primitives who fall down dead at the sight of a sacred person even if it's their own cousin. But when they showed up he began to shake, like this. He was shaking so hard he thought he was going to shake himself right out of his car and across the street on his hands and knees. They didn't see him and he got away. He got back across the bridge all right because those Triumphs drive themselves. Then he came over here. I thought he came to kill me because it was me who brought Martin Vandersen into his life. I was afraid he had a weapon on his person, like a lady's ivory-handled revolver that belonged to his grandmother, maybe with a blood-red ruby in the handle. The rich kill you with the very best, it's a matter of noblesse oblige. So I pleaded with him for my life, I said 'Martin Vandersen's relieved you of a life-threatening wife.' I said 'Unless that's what you want, an early death with her kneeling by you, floor, street, wherever, so the last thing you see is her beloved face.' That was too much to think about so he toppled over. But before he fell asleep he told me his manuscript was in his car and he was going out to the beach to burn it. I said, 'Why don't you do it in your fireplace?' and he said, 'The smell of human flesh. The neighbors will call the cops.' If he talks that way in his novel it's good he's burning it."

The bitter brew fumed up over the percolator lid.

"You ever see that painting *Paradiso*?" he asked them, bringing black coffee in chipped mugs. "Where everybody's dressed up in their Renaissance best, finding each other again, falling into each other's arms? Well, the people in that paradise are forever in the shape in which they were last seen on earth. There're people of all ages, kids and middle-aged ones and old, old ones. I've always puzzled over that painting, it wakes me up in the middle of the night. I think, Well, it's all right for the young, it's real nice to spend the rest of eternity looking the same. But what about the older ones? I bet when they get a little time to be alone up there and to think, maybe the old ones say to themselves 'It was me at six years old and it was me at twenty and it was me at forty, so why does it have to be me forever when I was ninety-one? Why ninety-one forever even if my arthritis is all gone?' Myself, if I could have a word with God, I think I'd tell him 'Look at me, God. I'd hate to go through eternity like I am now at forty or like I'm going to be, even worse. I resemble a bullfrog now, my chin is adhering to my chest because you took my neck away, and look at my sad froggy eyes. I used to be good-looking, God. I was good-looking for a long enough time to give *you* time, God, to think about keeping me that way forever.' "And to the host, who had scalded his mouth with the hot coffee and was bent over in pain, head down to his knees. "I'm telling you this as an argument for an early death. You ought to make it up there before you look any worse. Maybe all you need to do to get there fast is persuade your wife to come back to you."

No one spoke, not even Claud, on the drive to the ocean. They went in Claud's rattling car and, by a trick of his, the manuscript lay in Ilona's lap. Its weight was impressive. She guessed there must be close to a thousand pages in the brown wrapping paper tied with string. No matter if he had revealed nothing more than his own confusion, and how trapped he was in his own life and how oblivious to the rest of the world, no matter—his pages ought not to be burned. Why, then, was she riding along with the manuscript in her lap?

Claud slowed down along the Great Highway, selecting the site with care. On the landward side of the highway the old houses and the new stucco motels faced the sea, and on the seaward side the high sand dunes, some ten feet high with purple iceplant clinging to their slopes, belonged somewhere else on the earth, an ancient port on a desert coast.

Claud parked before a green stucco motel aglitter with specks of gold. She was about to say *No, not here* and said nothing. Martin's house had stood there, and she knew that when the pages had all gone up in smoke and they were climbing back over the dune, Claud would pause at the top and say *You know, I think Martin's basement was along about here. In fact, right there. You see that green motel?* And the specks of gold would be flashing and sparkling in the rays of the setting sun.

"Somewhere else," she said, "might not be so windy."

"No wind anywhere," Claud said, and got out first.

They climbed the dunes and were met by a fitful wind, the ragtag end of a storm yesterday. The wind, though not strong enough to break up the glaring overcast sky, was lifting foam high off the breakers. A fisherman in hip-high rubber boots was casting his line into the breakers, a very small figure in the glare of sky and water. Far down the beach a few persons and a dog were either approaching or retreating in the mist along the water's edge.

Claud led the way down the slope, past three seated figures facing the sea. It was obvious in their calmness, the disciplined erectness of their backs, that they were meditating. Ilona, trudging down last, saw they did not move a muscle. It was as if no one passed by. Up ahead, Claud stopped at the foot of the slope, turned, and waved his arms. The spot he had chosen was only a few yards from the three figures who were seated in an arc, above.

"Why here?" Jerome asked. "Look, there's nobody for miles."

"These dudes don't see a thing," Claud assured him. "They won't laugh at you, they won't cry. They're above it all, they're floating above all human suffering. You used to be into it yourself."

The figure in the middle was a girl, her long hair drawn back, her face blanched by the cold, her heavy clothes shapeless. The young man to the south of her was bearded, his dark hair hanging thickly to his shoulders, and the young man to the north was beardless, his wisps of thin blond hair lifted and laid down by the wind, his eyes closed. The other two held a steady gaze on the horizon.

"We're disturbing them," she said.

"We can't. Nothing can." Claud took the package from her and dropped it straight down at his feet. The package scooped a shallow place for itself, scattering sand over his boots.

They searched a long way, up and down the beach, for enough dry sticks and driftwood. From far Ilona saw Jerome moving about, a figure in an excellent suit a shade darker than the sand. He stumbled over a mound, and she expected to see him drop to his knees and stay there. A dog, running along the beach in zigzags and loops, stopped to nose the package and dig furiously with its hind legs, throwing sand over it. They came back with their arms full.

With a show of expertise, Claud arranged wood and newspapers and set the pile ablaze with Jerome's cigarette lighter. "The rest is up to you. Don't throw it all in at once,

94

you'll smother the fire. A few pages at a time and don't try to read them."

Kneeling, Jerome untied the string, unfolded the wrapping. The wind lifted the top page and began to slip it away, left it to riffle through the pages just underneath. Then, leaping up, waving his arms, he was shouting at the three figures above them. "Look what's going on here, fellas!"

He took off running, he ran in circles, searching for something he must have seen earlier, and swooped down on it at last—a yellow plastic pail, or part of a pail. Waving it above his head, he ran down to the water, waded in, filled the pail, ran back and past the fire, and stopped before the girl.

"Fellas, look!" he shouted, holding the pail over his head. "I'm going to burn myself up. I'm like your Buddhist monk over in Saigon. See! I'm pouring this gasoline over myself. See, fellas?"

Ilona saw no change in the faces of the three, no smiles, not even annoyance. The one with his eyes closed did not open them, and the other two continued to gaze out to sea.

Jerome tipped the pail and the water splashed over the crown of his head and streamed down his face. He threw the pail away, leaped down the slope, ripped off his shoes and socks, and thrust his bare foot into the fire. He kept his foot in the fire beyond the limits of even Claud's endurance.

Claud shoved him off, and he went hopping away. Hopping back, he picked up the entire manuscript and dropped it into the fire. The fire was almost extinguished. Sparks, burning bits of wood shot out all around. Claud handed him a long stick, and he stirred the fire to life again. The flames flared up, the corners of the pages turned brown, curled up, the words in black ink turned brown and lost their meanings. The top pages rippled, rose up and fell back and vanished, and the pages below, facing suddenly the vast white sky, shriveled into evanescent shards. The bulk of the manuscript remained almost untouched, too heavy and dense for the air to enter and lead the way for the flames.

Jerome limped away fast and Ilona followed him. For a long way he waded through shallow water, cooling his burned foot. His trousers were wet to the knees. She could tell by his back, by his lifted shoulders and bent head, that he was crying. In the white glare of sky and ocean she lost sight of him. When she found him again he was sitting on the sand, up away from the water, gripping his ankle.

She sat beside him. The skin on the sole of his foot was burned away. "That monk," he said. "I wasn't ridiculing him. God no. I wish I were him. The man had something to burn himself up for. God no. The world's over there, that's where it's at, and I thought it was waiting to hear what's going on inside my head. The rot up here, up here. What I did in that novel to her and old Neely, Willy Nilly Neely, poor old cocksman! You look at your pages, you look at the type, it's like barbed wire. You've got your victims, your prisoners inside there. Years ago I read about what

96

those syndicates down in Mexico do to the prostitutes who try to escape. They roll them up in barbed wire. I was doing that to her. Elisa."

The wind was colder, it seemed colder. It stung her face, hung back, slipped by, came around and struck her face again. She could say that the ones he thought he'd imprisoned behind barbed wire were not there, that he had imprisoned only himself and not forever, and someday he would forgive himself for the attempt on their lives and his own, but the roar of the ocean filled the sky and her voice would be unheard.

"Well, I guess I set them free," he said. "I guess I'm free myself, free of her, free of her boy. He always reminded me of his father. I think I loved that boy, I think he loved me, but I'm glad he's gone. I loved his father, too, but he shook me up, the son of a bitch. But I can't say I'm free of Martin Vandersen. Maybe I'll never get rid of him, maybe I'll become one of those nighttime teeth-gnashers, and if I ever get married again my wife will sleep in a separate bed. The only way I can ease myself of him is to imagine him when he's old, you know what I mean? When he's old and his fame was brief and his hair was brief, all those seraphic curls gone, all those red curls shining under all my goddamn lamps, and his seraphic cheeks deflated, and his body shrunken, the way when you're old you shrink down to half your size, and he's deaf, maybe, one of those smiling old deaf men who don't know they can't hear. Maybe we'll embrace in para-

97

dise. 'Goddamn, Martin, glad to see you looking so old!'
Maybe that's where we were in a dream I had a couple of
nights ago, but I didn't know that's where until Claud reminded me there's a paradise. Joe Neely was there, too, and
we were standing on a sort of balcony, the three of us, me
and Neely and Martin. We had on white robes like angels or
maybe they were hospital nightgowns, but we weren't old
yet, we were like we are, or Neely was, and all the pain and
envy and anger were gone, and there were all these women,
down below, women and children looking up at us, and I
said to Martin or he said to me or Neely said to him or to me,
one of us said it anyway, 'Which one did you say was Elisa?'
We didn't know and it didn't matter. Maybe that dream
made me decide to burn the stuff."

It was a long way back to the fire. He walked all the way
in the shallow water, limping. The three meditators were
gone, the fishermen gone. The only ones left were a lone
figure far down the beach and Claud, poking the fire.

"It's got to be ashes," Claud said. "You don't want somebody to come along and read a fragment and take it home.
It could trouble him the rest of his life—What came before
and what came after?" At the end of his stick the last page
burst into flame.

They climbed the sand dunes, Claud in the lead, and at
the top he paused. The green motel was flashing a million
promises of glamour and ecstasy to the overcast day. No
blazing sunset was necessary.

98

"Claud, don't say it," she begged.

Jerome came up the dune last, shoes in hand. His hair was wet, his trousers wet, his face pinched closed by the cold wind and the loss of his captives. A white line, like salt, sealed his lips.

They went down the sand dune together, no one leading, no one straggling, and all the way back into the city they spoke not one word.

# 13

One night she heard Martin's footsteps on the stairs. She knew they were his footsteps, always light, rather slow, those of someone led by a reason not yet known to him. The room where she slept and where she wrote faced the landing. The lamp was on, the curtains closed. He tapped at the window.

"Ilona? It's me."

It began, the trembling of desire and resistance to it. Her

hand was trembling so much she had trouble with the simple lock.

Avoiding the room where the lamp was lit, he went on into the kitchen.

"You're working late."

She was wrong about his footsteps. He knew why he had come. He was troubled over what she was doing in her own way about the end of love. Or, as usual, she was only imagining what went on in someone else's eyes.

"It's not about us," she said.

Relief in his eyes, and then a doubt, and then, perhaps because he chose not to doubt her, his eyes accepted her words. "Some say it's best to wait ten years before you say anything about any experience. If you did that you'd give me time to escape and yourself, too, if you want to escape."

Was he cautioning her to wait until balance was restored by time, to wait until the memory of love would suffice to soothe her and redeem her? She had only to wait and wait.

"What's it about, then?"

"It's about my brother."

"I forgot," he said. "I forgot you had a brother."

Strange that this man by leaving her was leading her more deeply into herself than he had when he was with her in those few years of love. Like a guide who has no idea where he leads.

"That's what I tried to do," she said. "I tried to forget

him, but I couldn't. I was always afraid he would appear, knock at my door just as it was getting dark, when we were sitting down to supper or when it was just getting light and the air was cold, and I would be left alone with him because everyone would leave me, even you, not my child but maybe even her, and my friends, my few friends. He'd knock and I'd open the door and I'd see his face again, his face that never knew how it looked to the world. It's about him, even if it's just for myself to see, because now he breaks my heart."

"Ilona." He came no closer. She wanted him to come closer but he stayed where he was, across the room. "Ilona, can you see me that way? Not like everybody else sees me. Not like you see me now. You think I'm blessed, you think Somebody out there loves me, and sometimes I go along with that because it feels good. But I'll tell you something. Someday I'm going to be back with everybody else again, you won't be able to tell me apart. Me, just a lowly human being again, maybe even lowlier than the rest, and what if I knock at your door, the real Martin Vandersen, Old Mortal Martin? Would I break your heart?"

When he came to her she put her hands over her face to hide her desire for him. He kissed her hands hiding her face and led her back down the hall that was not wide enough for two abreast, and drew her down onto her bed. She had imagined herself far in his past, faded from his memory, and she was engaged, day and night, in a desperate rescue of herself, a rescue by thought, by words, but all the time she had known the rescue required something more—his body over hers, his hands over her, his mouth over her, his desire moving over those secret places where proof of love seems to lie.

Apart, each facing upward in that rapt position memory places you in years later: "Ilona, did I tell you I dreamed about you? The other night? You knew where underground rivers ran and where trees could be planted and thrive."

Nights to come, when she was to be wakened by her fear of belonging nowhere, by despair over who she was, so lacking in the virtues that make your presence, your time on earth so precious to some others, it was to calm her like a deep persuasion of his love.

# 14

At dawn when the phone rang she was lying against his back, curved to him as she had been curved to him countless times before, and in the first moments of waking the loss of him had not yet come about. Wrapping his shirt around her—it was closest to hand—she ran down the hall, praying that all was well with everyone.

The sound of distance like little waves, and within the waves a voice asking to speak to Ilona Lewis.

"That's me," she said. "I'm here."

Washed over by distance, the voice—a man's voice or the grainy voice of an elderly woman clerk—told her that her brother, Albert Lewis, had died at six that morning. A voice in a vast hospital told her that her brother had been brought there in the night, suffering a heart attack.

"I'll come on the earliest plane," she said, and when she put down the phone her cries were the ones her brother kept down in his throat that last morning when he came to the bedroom door to beg her to allow him to protect her from the world.

Martin sat on the rim of the tub and bathed away the sheen over her body. He drove her to the airport and, waiting in line to board the plane, she rested her head against his chest and he kissed her on the brow, and to everyone else he must have appeared to be someone who would be waiting for her when she returned.

# 15

A glass door to a dim vestibule, and the landlady peering out at the woman on the porch who had pressed the bell so early in the morning.

"I'm Albert's sister." At last. And when she was let in she said it again, repeating it to exonerate herself from the years of her denial of it.

A second, inner vestibule, dim also, a black pay phone on the wall and a black leather discard chair before it. So this was where he sat waiting for her to call at the time they had

agreed upon by letter, and always he had waited half an hour
in advance, afraid he would miss her call or another tenant
would have claimed the phone. So this was the small space
wherein he waited for her voice.

"Come in. You like cuppa tea?" *I have a Greek landlady
who knows how to make repairs like a man.*

Ilona followed her into the flat and down the long hallway
and into the kitchen. The presence of the night still lay
heavily in the rooms off the hallway, they were so solidly
crowded with massive furniture and the drapes were closed,
but the light of day came through the kitchen window.

"Your brother a nice guy. Nice guy. He always like cuppa
tea. Sit down."

Ilona sat at the table, in the chair where her brother had
sat. A large dog dropped a red ball at Ilona's feet and backed
away, head cocked, a bright anticipation in the corners of its
eyes. Its black and white fur lay in tidy layers like the thick,
tended hair of a caricature musician.

"Your brother, he like Hector. He always throw the ball.
Nice guy."

The sister, too, threw the ball. She threw it the length of
the hall and the dog was back in no time, dropping the ball
at her feet again. She threw the ball again, keeping her eyes
on the dog to avoid the landlady's eyes. This woman's two
sons, both in their teens when her brother moved in, became doctors while her brother went on living in the same
room, observing their transformation with a tenant's pride.

"He talk alla time about his sister. Come in, have cuppa tea, I say. He say, Thank you, thank you, and talk alla time about his sister. He want you to come here so he can take care of you. You got no husband?"

"Not now."

"How you make a living?"

Not very well—she could say that if the time were appropriate to smile. Not very well, but enough of a living to keep a roof over herself and her child, and the pitcher of milk was always full, surprisingly, as if by a benediction, the same as that bestowed on the couple in the myth whose wine jug or milk jug was miraculously full for the rest of their lives because they'd shared their meager fare with a couple of strangers.

"Albert tells me you write alla time."

"That was a long time ago"—lying to clear away the scornful curiosity trembling in the landlady's eyes, the derision of this sister who failed to attend to reality. But some lies, like riptides, sweep you out into a dangerous truth. If she had hoped to go on dreaming up enough stories to keep the pitcher full or partway full for the rest of her life, that hope, fragile anyway, must have left her when Martin left.

"The sweet ladies, you know about them? Bernice and Harmonia? Oh, they got sweet voices. Lady angels. They come to visit him, they take him for nice rides. They tell me Albert loves the Lord. They talk alla time about Lord Jesus. They smile at me like I got a pain."

"He told me." His voice a loud whisper, he had told her about the two ladies. Though it was unthinkable, his whisper implied, the ladies might be closer to God than she was. Sunday dinners at their house, reading aloud from the Bible, each taking a turn, and she had imagined his voice— portentous, hollowy, shaky with awe.

Ilona, like a bird that leads the predator away from her nest, eluded the landlady's eyes prying after an incontrovertible sign of sorrow. The sweet ladies had borne him in their angel arms, but where was his sister? The sister had kept her distance, hoping that her sorrow over him, already deep when she was a child, when she had no name for it, would serve as her presence near him, and knowing that it would not.

"Where's Al now?"

She mistook it for a superstitious query and looked into the woman's eyes to see where her brother was in the woman's own scheme of the world. Did this landlady think he was still in this room where he drank his tea and threw the ball and talked about his sister?

"What you going to do with his body?"

She had always to gather her strength to answer any questions, the ones asked and the ones unasked, and this one required of her a strength to overcome the shame of her failure to appear before he became only a body. "Yesterday afternoon," she began, knowing the landlady was listening to the shame stumbling around in her voice and not to the words, "as soon as the plane got in I went out to the hospital and tried to find the doctor who was on duty when he was brought in. Somebody said he'd be back soon and I waited but he didn't come back and then I walked for miles up and down the corridors, trying to find somebody who could tell me how to get my brother out of there." Up and down the corridors—it had the sound of pity for herself, but she had felt none. Some fault of hers, like a lack of foresight, kept her in narrow corridors, unable to escape, unable to suggest a way of escape for anybody she might run into there.

"What you going to do with him?"

The same question. It had to be answered with a word of such terrible finality she could barely hear herself saying it. But the landlady heard.

"The Greeks, we bury our dead."

It must seem to this woman that what she, the sister, was to do with her brother's body would be her final failing of him—this complete vanishing as if he had never lived. But the ancient Greeks built pyres, didn't they? Isn't that what all peoples did, in ancient times? And the ones who became ashes were remembered, weren't they? The millions who vanished into ashes in the concentration camps were re-membered, weren't they, and the ones everywhere in the world who were dragged away in the night were remem-bered, weren't they, though they disappeared without a trace? Each one by someone or all by someone?

"Alla time, your brother walk, walk alla time," the landlady said. "Restless, always walk. I tell him he going to wear out all those shoes he got. He laugh at me, he tell me he got enough shoes to last one hundred twenty years."

# 16

With the key to her brother's room in her hand, a dimestore key that might open any door in this place except the land-lady's door, Ilona climbed the rubber-tread stairs to the second floor, passed along a gray-walled hallway, by several doors close together, and unlocked her brother's door. She left the door open, to breathe.

The room was a cell and the smallness gripped her heart, confirming for her, once and for all, how small it had always been, her heart. She had imagined the room larger, of

course. You always imagine comforts for someone you fail
to comfort. Above his cot a cardboard sign, printed with
blue pencil:

> Turquoise Bulletin Board
> Third Revised Notice
> as of May 14, 1969
> In an Emergency Please
> Notify my Sister
> Ilona Lewis

Over the erasures of previous numbers, her present phone
number was printed in red.

> If the above number proves to be
> in error, the correct number can
> be located in my wallet. Signed,
> *Albert L. Lewis*

The odor of sweat, the lingering odor of life. The cot and
dingy blankets, a kitchen chair, a dresser, and half the cell,
the back part, taken up by clothes on hangers hooked over
lines that stretched from wall to wall. Only the top of a
grimy window and the upper part of a closet door were visible above the lines of clothes. Always, his desire for clothes
imbued with the lives of other men, garments that must
have been, for him, like gifts left for a son by many kindly
fathers, left for a nephew by generous uncles. He must have
imagined them watching over him from high windows, so

pleased their clothes were being put to further use by this sensible and grateful man.

Long gray underwear over the back of the chair, and on the seat of the chair a box filled with ties in a snakepit twining. Under the dresser, oxblood oxfords, black moccasins, a pair of white buck shoes that must have belonged to a church-going man, three hundred pounds. She remembered his slender bare feet, the tendons, the tension, the unpredictability of those bare feet on the bare floorboards at night.

"Throw everything over the railing."

With an armload of plastic bags the landlady moved swiftly around her, dropping the bags on the cot, and, into one, stuffing the tenant's long underwear, a large bundle of socks from the dresser drawer, the ties, a suit and four sweaters along with their wire hangers, exposing behind the first row of clothes a portion of the second row.

"Follow me."

Down the narrow hallway and out onto a railed porch, a balcony of sorts. The stairs down to the yard were boarded up, the drop to the earth, to the damp, bare yard was twenty feet or so. The landlady lifted the heavy bag to the rail and gave it a push. Over and down. The bag split on impact with the hard earth and the clothes leaped forth. A shoe kicked out, a sleeve and a pantsleg jerked once.

"Throw everything over. Is okay. I go down and make a pile."

Briskly the landlady went back along the hall toward the front of the house. On the ground floor there would be a rear door to her flat and she would emerge into the yard. In an unknowable maze you have to imagine an exit.

Under the cot, four pairs of overshoes, elaborately large and all readily available for the coming winter that he was not to enter. She gathered them up from the strings of dust and placed them in the bottom of a plastic bag. Flannel pajamas, thin as gauze in spots, from the foot of the cot, and from the first row of hanging clothes an apple green cardigan sweater, a stained winecolor robe, steelgray trousers crudely darned, three gaudy shirts that once belonged to a racetrack buff, and three suits for summer. The bag was too heavy to lift from the top. She lifted it from the bottom and carried it down the hallway to the porch.

Below in the yard the landlady was gathering the scattered clothes into a pile. Seen from above, she was even more plump, shorter, and the weak sunlight showed the black dye in her twisted-back hair. She looked up to see if the sister had appeared, their eyes met, and the quick, wavering light in the landlady's eyes was an accusatory question: *Since you failed to come and see him, can you see at all?* Ilona rested the bulging bag on the rail and pushed it over.

The bag plummeted in an instant, smacking the hard earth and flying apart. Up to that moment her abandonment of her brother had been a secret unknown in its extent even to herself. Now it became a public act, though no one looked out from the windows of the tenement next door, not from any grimy window of the four stories nor from the basement windows whose sills were level with the earth. No face stared out from the shreds of curtains. She knew the place had tenants, she had seen pale children playing in the entrance. But no one came to a window to see someone's earthly possessions strike the ground. Only the goad, the landlady, saw.

Up and down the hall, carrying out to the rail bags filled with sweaters, shirts, towels, brushes, combs, empty coin purses, half a hundred of them filled only with hope, and carrying over her arms suits for summer and suits for winter, and when all the hanging garments were cleared away and the clotheslines taken down, the closet was accessible.

Someone in an adjacent room was watching television or listening to the radio; she heard the boxed-in voices. The man struck the air; she heard the rustle of his arm and the shout of rage. Other persons so close around her brother— had their sounds comforted him, even the sound of someone endangered by his own self?

On the closet floor, her father's black leather suitcase, familiar as a repetitive dream. Along with the cardboard boxes tied with twine the suitcase had gone aboard the mailman's truck, then aboard the train to Seattle, and when their aunt died it was loaded aboard the train to Chicago. He had gone east when everyone else was going west. He had gone back into the city of his mother's childhood, transforming it into the city of his future, imagining his mother a little girl again in a doorway not far from his own. What a sight he must have been on that train! Trembling with courage, loudly sociable with the person next to him in the coach like a jocular, seasoned traveler. The passengers must have been warily entertained by him, by his voice, by his clothes, by his anxious, excited face, by the way he bent low over his meal, guarding it from the covetous. If she had accompanied him on that train, obliged by her heart to sit next to him, her dear, dread companion, how she would have longed to sit far away from him, denying him even a brief acquaintance, her face turned toward the passing sights.

Down on her knees she opened the suitcase. The figured paper lining was a dry brown like the manuscript pages before they flamed up. The World Atlas, here again, already old when she was a child, its maps even then in wrong shapes, and here again was his geography textbook, and the arithmetic textbook, and the grammar, and the dimestore tablet over which he had bent his head so low, his face so close to his hand erasing an error, erasing one small letter into extinction, leaving a hole where the offender had been. Over the tablet pages his pencil, sent along the blue lines at his father's command, pressed factual information of extreme importance to the world.

The earth turns on its axis from west to east once every twenty-four hours, giving us the impression that the sun moves around the earth from east to west. The

earth completes one rotation of 360 degrees in a day;
hence in one hour it must rotate 1/24 of 360 degrees or
15 degrees.

The Bible, here again, in its flexible leather cover, with its
red silk cord to slip between the pages. They belonged to no
church, no temple, but their father had made them read the
Bible, and was it to blame for her delusion that everything
that happened on earth was taken into a divine memory?
There was no memory like that.

Objects both strange and familiar, the way sacred objects
seem. The gray photograph folder, here again, embossed
with the name of the studio and *Chicago*. If she opened it
she'd find a full-length portrait of a young woman before
she became their mother. The pale, pure oval face, the eyes
bravely meeting the camera's eye, dark hair drawn up and
her dress outgrown, lace cuffs barely concealing thin wrists.
If she were to look into that face would she find there the
secret disquiet that must have come later to the mother's
face, the forbidden wondering over the end of her children's
lives—when and where? Here again, the pocket planetar-
ium her father had invented, a square of cardboard folded
in sections and tied with a string. If she were to unfold it,
the sun and the planets would spring into existence, surprisingly white on the black background of space. Once or
twice he had mused over a desire to visit Einstein, and when
he died away from home she wondered if he were on his way

to pay that visit and to unfold his modest design of the heavens under that great man's gaze. They were small enough, these possessions, to fit into her purse and small enough to be hidden away when she got home, where she would promise them to take them out later.

Only the dingy blankets, the flat sepia pillow, and the limp sheets that would be sure to rip were he to lie down on the cot one more night, only these were left to throw over the rail. His last night on this cot—he hadn't known it was his last, and this unknowing was like a trick played on him, a humiliation, the last, the deepest, the most mysterious of all the deprivations of his life, the ones known to him and the ones he could never even suspect.

On the porch for the last time she looked out over the neighborhood at the roofs, the few, low trees, the mist that indicated where the lake must be. The landlady was in the kitchen, fixing supper for her husband, who would be home soon. It had taken a day to clear out the accumulation from almost twenty years in that room and the things from the stucco bungalow. Her brother had brought her here at last to this high porch above a damp yard where his possessions lay in a large, darkening heap.

The dust of the room over her clothes, her hair, her hands, she locked his door. There was no use in trying to rid herself of the dust before she went out into the city. Her hands refused to do anything about it anyway. Back along the hallway, past flimsy, narrow doors close together, through fumes

119

of menthol from behind one door, down the rubber-tread stairs and into the vestibule with the pay phone on the wall and the chair with a broken leather seat. She would come back tomorrow, to bid the landlady good-bye and to find the pastry cook and thank him for caring for her brother.

Out on the sidewalk the cold of early evening got through her raincoat, the advance cold of the coming winter. She had no heavy coat, she had never owned one or wanted one, nor any clothes other than a couple of skirts, a couple of blouses, a sweater, wanting no more than a few things easily carried to the capitals of the world and its far outposts, everywhere she had never been. She had wanted to be invisible—that was another reason for only the few possessions. Invisible, moving among people everywhere, observing all particulars and no one able to observe her.

On the bus she looked out at the streets familiar to her brother, at the cafés where he sat at counters, friendly to proprietors and waitresses, imagining himself a man of the world always on the verge of a momentous occasion. The bus entered the park, a prosperous section where lamps were already lit in the entrances of high apartment buildings, the glimmering lights restoring shades of gold to the twilight trees, and she imagined him striding through this park like someone on a mission of historical consequence, or like a large skimming bird keeping up with the bus. Unless he had slowed down toward the end, lamed by the pain in his heart, and then she saw that his face was not a young face anymore, that his vision of the world belonged to the face of an older man whom she might not recognize at first glance.

Along the boulevard by the lake the bus moved slowly through the glare and glitter of heavy traffic, and she saw him hurrying to a night job or homeward bound, a figure in several layers of other men's clothes, his heavy overcoat flapping in the wind, and a fedora, with a high-class firm's name on the silk lining, down low to his eyebrows. On the bridge over the dark waters reflecting the gold and silver lights of this downtown, he paused, imagining his sister beside him at the railing. *There, you see? It's Lake Michigan, you see?* pointing downward to make sure she wasn't looking for it in another direction.

# 17

Up in her unlit room on the hotel's fifteenth floor she drew apart the drapes to see a little more of this city at dusk. The gray building across the street seemed a surprising reflection of the one she was standing in, but, locating the window at a level with hers, she found no reflection of herself. An adamantine sightlessness was in all things and in all creatures, and she was probably the last one to learn this. For too long a time, when even a moment was perilous, she

had allowed herself the delusion that there was sight everywhere, in everything.

She closed the drapes and lay down, face up, raincoat
on, and exhausted as a penitent after a journey across a continent on foot, she wept and the tears streamed down her
temples. For years, what a mighty struggle went on in that
cell of a room! All the clothes of other men taking up the
space that fear over his abandonment would have claimed,
the fear that if given a chance would have filled up that cell
completely.

She slept in her clothes on top of the spread and was wakened by her desire to see her child and to hear the girl's voice
that, just by its sweet vivacity, would assure the mother she
was a good person after all, despite any evidence to the contrary, and even someone who could bestow a blessing. But
even if she were able to put in a call to so far a place, her child
had heard of the mother's brother only once or twice, not
enough times to know he truly existed. The only way she
could tell about him now was to say *Antonia, I wanted to tell
you I love you*, and the child would think the mother was
nowhere else but home, waiting for *her* to come home. Unless she heard the sorrow under those words of love and
would be a little afraid of what was kept quiet when love was
voiced. She could call a friend, a woman back in San Francisco, a friend who had confided in her for years, but she
had told that friend nothing about her brother. Martin was

her confidant and one confidant was enough. She could tell only Martin about this entanglement of grief, but he was not at home, he was over on the mountain, lying in love through the afternoon.

She bathed and lay down again, wanting to sleep until morning, wanting not to wake up in the middle of the night and set Martin's phone to ringing in an empty house.

Footsteps along the corridor wakened her. She heard a door being unlocked and heard a woman's voice, buoyant, and heard a man's voice, low, and then the closing of the door. It was two o'clock in the room, it was midnight on the coast, and the imagined bliss of lovers brought on again the dying away of herself. It lasted only a few moments, because the dying away of her brother forbade her to die away over such a trivial reason as the loss of a lover. Even if she were surrounded by lovers, even if every room was intended for lovers, if in all the rooms around her lovers were lying together now for the first time, loving through the night, inseparable, she was forbidden to die away from their midst.

She brought her hand before her eyes, trying to see it as Martin had seen it that day, out in the sun and wind. Maybe he had called it beautiful just for its striving to form something of beauty, no matter how meager the results, how riddled with faults, and maybe he had known that the striving would save her from himself. If, for a time, you weren't a lover, there were other ways to belong in life. Like her brother in his cell filled with the clothes of a hundred other men, in the cell of her mind she'd striven to become so many others and in that way belong and in that way dispel a little of the vast abandonment the world casts on everyone's face.

# 18

The fortress like an old-time gangster's mansion where her brother lay—she went there again in the morning. She waited again at the heavy door with its high, round, opaque window like a blind eye. He must have passed this fortress countless times on errands of utmost importance for his future. Her first visit, the evening of the day she arrived, a man had peered out at her through the blind eye before he let her in. He wasn't expecting anyone and he wore a green shirt and green plaid trousers. This morning he was attired in a black suit, clothes for a busy day.

She told him her brother's name in case he had forgotten she had signed a permission for him to claim her brother's body at the hospital. He asked now, "Is he a tall fellow?" and then he remembered. Again she went up the wide, carpeted staircase, past shaded chapel rooms, holding her breath. If she were to let her breath go it would be irretrievable.

Upstairs at his desk he asked her, "Where do you wish to scatter the ashes?"—a whisper of false sympathy. "By the lake?" She shook her head. The lake waters were lead gray, miasmic, though people fished along its banks. "We often scatter the ashes over the cemetery." There was something absurdly futile about that. "The forest preserve?" She had seen no forest preserve anywhere near this scorched and moldy city, but she nodded.

Then she waited while the man flurried around behind a door to a small room. She hadn't yet seen her brother, and when the door was opened for her and the man stepped aside and she went in, at once the sense of her own life was lost to her in punitive imitation of her dead brother.

Under a sheet, only his head and feet exposed. Sparse black and gray tendrils of hair lay over his head, the dark curls gone. His nose was more curved, the nostrils more flared as if by all the odors and fragrances of his life. His feet, pointing outward, were very pale, the nails like discolored ivory, and the loneliness she had underestimated to save herself was now in its pure state. No agitation, no supplication led her away from that loneliness. She kissed his brow to tell him that in the years apart she had loved him deeply despite the obstacle that was himself, and expecting the film of sweat, the same as the day they parted, she was surprised to find his brow cold and dry. Whatever her kiss meant to her, for him it was of no consequence, placed on his brow an eternity ago.

Out in the sun again, she went on toward his street, assailed by the memory she had tried to keep away, of her brother striking their mother to the floor, and of herself, a child at the window watching him stride away, and wishing—afraid to pray for so awful a thing—that he would die someway, out there away from home. Yet they had loved him and he had wept and they had not sent him away, and as the years went by the turbulent youth gave way to the childlike man, but always the pariah, futilely camouflaged by all those clothes of all those other men who seemed to belong to the earth.

The closer she got to his street, the more articles of clothing lay along the curbs and in empty lots. They may have been there yesterday, even always, but she hadn't seen them, just as yesterday she hadn't seen the many persons tenaciously adrift in these few mild days.

The landlady was in the vestibule, chatting with a white-haired woman coming slowly down the inside stairs, her cane feeling the way.

"Dr. Muller," the landlady said, introducing the woman and neglecting to name Ilona, simply "Albert's sister." Since the brother was gone, there was no necessity to ask or to remember the name of the sister. Like a calm, worldly physician, the woman smiled a half-smile of sympathy over the facts of life. *A wise old woman lives down the hall from me. She revealed to me that Franklin D. Roosevelt, also known as F. D. R., had seven illegitimate daughters. She is the youngest. Nobody knows about this, so please keep it under your hat.*

"The Salvation Army, they tell me 'No, thank you,' " the landlady said to Ilona. "They got too much stuff already. So we take Al's stuff to the corner. Lots of people like free stuff."

Ilona asked her where she could find the man who had taken care of her brother, and the man who answered her knock was graciously quick, uncritical of whoever it was on the other side of the door. Slight, he stood very erect as if his spirit drew him upward while age shrank his body, two opposing forces.

"I'm Albert's sister," she said. "I want to thank you for taking care of him."

"Please come in."

Ilona stepped into the room where her brother had lain

and been tended, a room larger than her brother's, tidy, with flowered curtains at the clean windows, a crocheted spread over the double bed, an armchair, small rugs, a cook-stove.

"I am so sorry about Albert," he said. "Always a good morning, always polite. We will all miss him."

The odd, solitary figure of her brother was always to be expected, around a corner, down a corridor, on the seat next to you, any place, and this man was telling her, without his knowing, that she was not to blame for her brother's alone-ness, that her brother was not unlike all the solitary others, everywhere and always, each one odd in the way his own loneliness dictated.

"Sit down, please."

She sat in the armchair and he told her he had been a pastry cook. He described the varieties of pastries and re-called the number baked each day for the guests of the hotel, and she saw that even such airy concoctions as pastry spirals in memory can sustain your esteem for yourself to the very end.

"Did you know," he asked, "that Ho Chi Minh was a pas-try cook in Paris? I've followed his career with great inter-est. I suppose I, too, could have been a general under the right circumstances."

At the door they shook hands. His hand was small and smooth and warm, and he told her how he had admired her brother for his good cheer and consideration of others and told her again that all the tenants would miss him.

She left the house then, the house whose atmosphere was her brother's presence and her own, together. She had been one among the tenants because of his constant longing to see her again, because of his voice confiding and pleading over the pay phone in the dim vestibule, because of the countless times he must have imagined her at his side, entering the house with him, this place he had found for himself courageously in a city halfway across the country.

The sky was overcast. It had been clear earlier in the day. Out in the street a man's large white shoe lay on its side. Along the sidewalk, before a row of grime-dark apartment buildings, she passed a rubber overshoe, a belt, a man's black shoe. A shirt hung over a stair-rail. Farther on, a mound of earth and rocks in a vacant lot changed into a tangle of clothes as she passed by, and to save her reason she thought— If they had not been there yesterday, all these scattered clothes, it didn't mean they were his for sure. In a puddle of water by the curb a tie floated, partly blackened by the water, partly shiny blue, the blue an inducement to the overcast sky to show its true color.

# 19

The rain began while she waited by the hotel for the airport bus, a cold drizzle after the spell of warm weather. Three months later she was to see a newspaper item about the record cold in this city, and she was to picture the ice and snow over the earth of the forest preserve. *Do you know where the forest preserve is?* she had asked the landlady in the vestibule, and the landlady had answered *If they say so, it's there*, suspecting perhaps that the sister doubted its existence even as she had wanted to doubt the existence of her brother.

The plane rose into the rain darkening the sky before twilight. The rain was left behind and the sky was alight again for a little while, and then night took over.

Up on the small screen, way forward in the cabin, a short documentary began. She watched without benefit of sound. A famous photographer in a large fur coat and hat to match was telling anecdotes about the celebrated ones whose photographs were as famous as the persons themselves. One after the other their faces appeared. The rotund face of a Pope whose name Ilona failed to remember, an old man's face lively with a little boy's pleasure over having his picture taken. The bland face of Eisenhower, gone before she could count the stars on his general's cap. Hemingway's face above a thick turtleneck sweater, like a sacrificial head on a platter. And oh! the very large sadness in Einstein's moist old eyes, the white strands of hair drawn up in cosmic amazement. The forever young head of John Kennedy, an earnest university debater. And oh! the lion head of Albert Schweitzer, like a marble sculpture of a god somewhere in the future. The coveted face of Bardot—*All is dross that is not Helen*. Churchill's old toad face, a toad vexed by the weight of the jewel in its head. Claud would look like that in another twenty years. Again, the photographer in his grand fur coat, relating interesting things she couldn't hear, and in a moment he, too, vanished and the screen was white and empty, and then it, too, vanished.

She gazed out at the night, but the faces on the screen remained before her eyes. They were always there before your eyes, whether you were awake or asleep, so highly visible were they. You could even assume they were among the blessed of the earth, if you wanted to, if that was your favorite delusion.

Across the aisle, the three close-cropped soldiers began a laughing jag together, shouts and spurts of laughter, waking her from shallow sleep. Then in the calm after, only murmurs here and there in the dim cabin, a dream began to surface, a dream from several nights ago, or weeks ago, that shocked her now with its meaning. She was with Martin in a small room and she was whispering *Don't let him in* but the door was open and her brother entered. Nothing could keep him away. He was a young man again but oh so different. A white skullcap was on his head, his eyes were lucidly dark, unseeing of them, seeing beyond them, and he was calm as he had never been, his being infinitely resigned. No tumult anymore, no frightful suppositions. He sat down in a chair against the wall, placed on the floor a portmanteau of a past century, and the room became a waiting room. He was on his way elsewhere.

Far below lay the endless bas-relief mountains, lead color, iron color. There must be a moon, ravine shadows were sharp, and she thought—If some persons were in the light, like the ones up there on the small screen, like Martin, like the woman he loved, like all those who were embraced wherever they went, it didn't follow that all the rest were lost to the dark. The young man in the dream was as vivid as her brother's body in the gangster's fortress.

# 20

It was after midnight when she climbed the stairs to her apartment. She had heard Martin's footsteps on these stairs that last night, and now she wished he was hearing hers and was drawn up from his chair or up from his bed and over to the phone, so that, when she turned the key in the lock, her phone would be ringing. The apartment was silent and remained silent.

On the kitchen table a little book lay face down, as if the lamplight had placed it there on the instant. Had she been reading at this table that night? Almost weightless in her hand, *Madeleine*, by André Gide. Martin had left it. Something would be underlined, a passage meant as a message to her. Often he, too, relied on the wiser ones of the world to describe his dilemmas. Ah, here it was, his borrowed message. She sat down, blaming her weariness on the days past, on the hours gazing down from a great height on the depthless solitude of earth, but knowing that the weariness was over messages offered in words. Everything uttered, everything written was a message she failed to comprehend and failed to act upon.

Her vision slipped here and there, first to the last passage and then to the first, her eyes trembling with all they had seen away from home.

It was a day like all the other days. I had need to look up a date for the memoirs I was then writing. I had asked her for the key to the secretary in her room where my letters were put away. . . . Suddenly I saw her become very pale. In an effort that made her lips tremble, she told me that the drawer was empty and that my letters had ceased to exist.

What did his wife say then? How did she explain herself?

After you left, I found myself all alone again in the big house you were forsaking, with no one on whom to lean, without knowing what to do, what to become. . . . I first thought that nothing remained but to die. Yes,

truly, I thought that my heart was ceasing to beat. . . .
I burned your letters in order to do something. Before
destroying them I reread them all, one by one. . . .
They were my most precious belonging.

And he, what did *he* do then?

For a solid week I wept.

Ilona laid her head down on the open book. What did
Martin hope for these underlined passages? Did he hope to
persuade her not to forget or deform or destroy whatever he
had entrusted to her of himself? Did he hope to persuade
her of his love though he wasn't around anymore to confirm
it? If she fell asleep where she was, not moving a muscle,
without any objection from any part of her body, would her
sleep be like a promise to him that she would do no harm,
neither to him nor to herself nor to love, and would her
promise be sensed by him, enabling him to sleep through
the night beside the woman, serenely?

# 21

Every day, the entire day, she wandered the city, walking miles through neighborhoods where she had never been, hoping that when she returned to the apartment the lovers would be gone and she would be alone again, alone with all those beings in her imagination who were waiting to exist, waiting to be given faces, desires, personal trinkets, far countries, oceans, foibles, failings, aches and pains, balance, voices, sacred silences, waiting to rescue *her*, their rescuer. But the lovers were always there when she returned, and out in the city, wherever she went, she was afraid that by some trick of fate she would encounter them, they would appear, strolling out from a shop, from a café, and she would be face to face with them, inescapably.

One day she saw the woman again. It happened in an Italian café not far from her apartment. Ilona was inside, sitting at one of the small round tables and facing the door. She chose to sit facing the door because if she sat with her back to the door the lovers might enter without recognizing her. The place was fragrant with coffee and steamed milk and pastries. The day was warm, the door open, and she began to hear the voices around her after so long a time of hearing only his voice and her own in memory, repeating their last words to each other. Obsession wears itself out or wears out its prey, the self—one and the same, and then the world around begins to make itself known again like a person returning after twenty years away, brimming with his own life. Then the woman was in the doorway, her little boy at her side, the woman she had seen only one evening and who, since then, she saw everywhere.

The patrons in the café faded away, along with their voices, along with the world. Then the woman saw her, their eyes met, and the wound opened unbearably wide because the woman's eyes must look into his while they loved, the woman's eyes were like a stage where all her life went on for him to see. The man who came up beside her wasn't

Martin, but the wound was not to be healed simply because Martin was elsewhere, even if he were never to lie in love again with this woman, even if he were to love a thousand others and forget this one. Ilona saw the man frown when the woman told him she had changed her mind about this café. Only a fraction of a minute had passed, he had locked the car in that time or stopped to glance into a shop window, and what could have caused her in so short a time to refuse to enter this place? He glanced around at the patrons, at Ilona, and found no one to suspect, no one he had seen before and no one to remember.

When Ilona looked up again they were gone. So close a resemblance between the woman and the man beside her—she saw it clearly now. The man was the brother whom Claud had told her about, a sculptor living in Italy, in Florence, and on his rapid way to fame. They were brother and sister reflecting each other's beauty. Years later, when Martin and the woman were married and living in Florence, Ilona was to dream of the three, the woman, her brother, and Martin, sitting side by side on a bench in a marble rotunda, the woman between the men, precious to them, protected by their love. They were troubled, they were waiting for a verdict, a parting—Ilona didn't know what. She was barred from their lives. She saw only that Martin and the woman were holding hands, fingers entwined, she saw that their love was deepened by sorrow, and she tried to pry their fingers apart, waking herself with a harsh cry of despair over herself, over who she had become—desirous denier, scourge.

Before she went out into the streets she gave them enough time to leave the neighborhood, and then she found the streets as unfamiliar as those in another city. It was as if she belonged nowhere, as if this city, this part of the earth was no longer accessible, as if the earth itself belonged now to the woman and to her brother and to Martin. She got lost deliberately, wandering until evening, afraid to enter the apartment because the lovers, waiting there, would seem more enduring than ever.

Above the narrow passageway the little green globe was lit, casting a patina over the bank of mailboxes all alike. A letter from her child was waiting for her. Climbing the stairs, she began to read by the light of the large, dim globe that hung above the courtyard, fascinated by the foreign envelope, by the handwriting, like a provincial who has never received a letter in her whole life.

Dearest Mother,

First of all I am perfectly well and hope you will tell me you are too. If you ever wake up in the middle of the night, I hope you remember to tell yourself you blessed me, so you can go back to sleep. One night you must have done just that. It was when we got lost, John and I, because he was in so much of a rush to start up into the mountains before the monsoons came. He got careless about the trails, he was in such a hurry, and we ended up high in the mountains but not where we should have been. It was beautiful even though we were lost. We camped on the shore of a Hindu sacred lake. There was a mist over the lake until sunset when the mist lifted and we saw how incredibly blue it was. It's hard to describe that blue. It was either a deep blue or a light blue, because the lake was so clear and reflective and deep. We were camped in a stone hut and we'd been out of food for three days. We built a fire and got rid of the leeches on us. We took off our clothes and hung them on a pole over the smoke, and the leeches dropped off, and we stood close to the fire and pulled the leeches off each other. That night I thought We're going to be all right because my mother just woke up and remembered she blessed me. Of course the time was different because of the time zones, but that didn't matter. The next day we hiked over the pass and weak, weak, weak, we came down through a forest fragrant with vanilla and into a valley covered with mist, where we heard bells and knew we were safe. We came to a hut and two boys were in there and they gave us eggs and yogurt and yak-butter tea. They directed us to their aunt's house in the village, where we could stay for the night. On our way down to the village we met a hippie washing his clothes in the stream. "Hi," he said. "I'm Harvey. I'm from New York." So you see, we weren't lost anymore.

When we were up in the mountains we couldn't see

143

the farther mountains because a mist was over everything, the way it is before the monsoons, but for about
five minutes the mist parted and we saw those terribly
high peaks far in the distance, and the wind was whip-
ping long snow banners off the tops. We were really
high, we had to take slow steps, the oxygen was so thin.

I am back now in Swayambhu in our little house,
two stories, with a view of the Kathmandu valley as the
storms blow in. The windows are only latticework and
open to the night air, and I burn Chinese mosquito
coils to keep the monsters out. Below the window is a
water buffalo and I brush my teeth and spit on his
back. He doesn't seem to mind. I walk around the hill
to the springs for our water, which I carry in an earth-
enware jug. Except Tuesdays when it's men's day.
Nearby is a Buddhist temple on top of a mount, with
the eyes of Buddha painted on the walls. Sacred temple monkeys with crazy faces live in the trees on the
mount. The priests wear orange robes and walk around
the mount, spinning their prayer wheels. The prayer
wheels are silver cylinders and inscribed on them are
the words Om Mane Padme Hum, something like
that, and the priests say these words as they go around,
and the words go up to heaven.

Mother, you ought to come here. You said it would
be like a rite of passage for me and you made it possible
for me to come here. You said you weren't ready yet for
your rite of passage. You said you'd have to invent your

own. Mother, you are a contrary person, like you used to call me. But I love you with all my heart, whoever you are.

I guess Martin is back by now, so kiss him for me and ask him how it feels to be a celebrity.

Your precious child,
*Antonia*

On the landing she finished reading the letter by the light from the evening sky and then it seemed that the same light, the same hour lay over the entire world, just as it had seemed on those summer evenings when she had taken the deepening blue as a promise that someday she would find herself far away from the stucco bungalow. For a moment now the earth was hers to know, even as it was known to everyone to whom the earth with all its wonders appeared to belong. A child out in the world can do that for you, can bring you to belong in the world yourself. With the key in the lock, with her hand on the key, she bowed her head against the door that she must open.

22

Like Martin's place by the ocean, this cottage on the sand trembled with resonance from the deep waters at its doorstep. She felt it at once. If the ocean were to rise up suddenly, a level rising with no warning, or if it were to come thundering over, the way Claud had described it that night of the party, not much of a house would be lost. Years after her year in that little house it was washed out to sea, the first house to go because it was the farthest out, and no trace was left, no fragments were swept up against the other houses built on sand. High tides, high winds, the winds piling up the water, a full moon at its closest point to earth, a point called perigee, and the earth at its closest approach to the sun—all forces joined together to sweep it away.

Claud carried in her possessions from his car. Offering the cottage to her for the year his former wife was to be away, he had described Ilona's move as a step into the world, but anyone who had ever roamed the world or crossed an ocean would laugh at the distance she'd come, only twenty miles north from the city, around the same mountain whose one side at night was ornamented with lights and whose side facing the sea was densely dark.

Wandering the small rooms through the horizontal light from the setting sun, she knew she had chosen to come to this place so that the constant presence of the lovers in her being, as implacable as figures in a dream and who would demolish her if she stayed any longer in that dream, might be overcome by the reality of the ocean, and she knew that her fear of the night ocean was to wake her even on calm nights and that she would switch on a lamp by her bed and lie in light for a little while. Lamplight in the middle of the night always seems to emanate from the other side of the earth.

Claud came into the bedroom where she was sitting on the floor, glancing through the record albums she had found

147

in the closet. The music was opera, the faces of the celebrated singers on the covers like masks laden with cosmetics
and fate.

"She thinks she's an opera singer," he said. "I mean she *is*
an opera singer but she's usually in the chorus. Once in a
while she gets to sing a few words by herself. She likes it
out here, she strolls along the sand singing above the din
and everybody thinks she's crazy. Her voice isn't beautiful
enough to compensate for everything that's wrong in her
life. I wish it were."

The bedroom was almost bare, the bed not quite a full
bed, too narrow for a husband also but just right for a lover,
a night or two. On the chest of drawers was a framed snapshot of Claud at the age of twenty or so—barefoot on a lawn,
thumbs hooked in the front pockets of his jeans.

"Some of my stuff is here," he said. "There's a little bit of
me under the bed. When I left I thought if my valuables
were under there it would be like I was there, and if she had
a lover in her bed, I could hear them. She'd like that."

From under the bed he pulled out the same sort of grocery box she'd found in her brother's room, the universal
grocery box, and the grating sound of sand came along with
it. He sat down on the floor beside her and brought up a pair
of bronze-plated baby shoes.

"They don't do this anymore," he said, weighing the
shoes in one hand. "It's like I died at the age of one."

A wristwatch, the crystal badly scratched, his initials and

the year of his graduation from high school engraved on the back. A battered book next.

"The name of the kid in here is Diamond. He sleeps in a stable loft and he has spells of delirium, and every time he's delirious he goes off in the arms of the north wind, who's a great big woman. That's the way I remember it, but it might not be that way." Over the inside of the cover, a drawing of a marvelously large woman, her hair flowing and rippling across the sky, and in her arms a very small, very thin boy. "She carries him off on excursions and the last time she doesn't bring him back. See, here's my name in the properly rounded letters, and my age. Claud McCormack, nine years old. This stuff, this watch, this book, these adorable shoes, I found in my mother's garage. The rest of the stuff, I'm to blame."

Up from the box a blue shirt, mottled with sweat and fuel oil. A pair of unwashed gray socks, holes in the toes and heels. A black wallet, split along the seams, and another wallet, yellow leather embossed with the Aztec calendar. A jockstrap. A half-smoked cigarette in an empty box of matches.

"My last cigarette."

A dozen and more ballpoint pens in a bundle, bound around with a rubber band. A mailbox, the kind that hangs on a wall, its coat of green paint flaked away. A red toothbrush, bristles flattened.

"All this junk, I've been saving it with a purpose in mind.

It's for that librarian who used to beg me for mementos of my life. Unless he's forgotten how he used to desire me. Some university library—Sore Neck, Nebraska, or Hang Dog, Georgia, I can't remember which. Anybody who's ever got one paltry word in print hears from him. He wants to embalm the writer's spirit. That's his word, embalm, not mine. You've sent him something?"

"I need it myself."

"Ilona, send him something. It might be the only way you'll be remembered. He stashes it away—manuscripts, underwear, prostheses, bounced checks, pisspots, empty bottles of sleeping pills, empty bottles of booze, condoms, he stashes it all away in a sort of tomb. No earwigs, no moths, no maggots, no mice, no rats, nothing ravenous. And think of it, Ilona—every hundred years your stuff gets set out on a revolving shelf in a glass case and round and round you go. I can't see how he can promise us that hundred years slot. Writers proliferate like rabbits. We'll be lucky to get on that merry-go-round every seven thousand years. What do you think, do you think seven thousand years from now when this junk goes around, along with my one novel and my picture on it, some beautiful girl will fall in love with me? Maybe by that time girls will have three eyes, but it won't matter how she looks as long as she falls in love with me. Like Anna for Dostoevski, only seven thousand years too late. Not just in love with my soul, but me, me, driving her wild in bed."

A pair of shoes, a grayed, rundown pair of canvas shoes, the shoestrings knotted together.

"They're not mine. I'll let him think they're mine. They belonged to a friend of mine, a fairly decent poet. The son of a bitch stepped out of these shoes and over the edge of a cliff, up in Mendocino. A couple of guys fishing on the rocks found his body. I was living on my boat at Fort Bragg and I went over to the cliff and found his shoes."

Swiftly he bent his head away, then he got up and drew her up. "Ilona, come to bed with me. Come in under with me."

That longing for another lover, that longing she confessed to herself reluctantly because the desire was like a betrayal of Martin, because it was an accusation that *she* was the deserter, that longing for a lover who would bring her to the bliss she imagined for those other lovers, who would take her down into that deep communion with all lovers, now that longing confessed itself to this man.

It was night when they lay apart. The ocean was louder. The sound of a breaking wave began at one end of the beach and traveled its length, and before the sound reached the other end another wave began to break. There was no silence between the waves.

"At night," he said, "I'll tell you how it is out there at night. Out there the clouds pile up on the horizon like that wave I told you about and I figure that's just what it is and everybody else has got the message over their crackly radios and they're already climbing the nearest mountain with their loved ones. But me, I'm sticking it out, smoking my dope, singing at the top of my voice. I can't keep a tune like my wife but I sing anyway. I sing what my father used to sing when he was shaving in the morning. 'Throw out the lifeline, someone is drifting away.' Or I sing, 'Kansas City, here I come, they got some crazy little women there and I'm gonna get me one.' The cabin's a mess, my bunk stinks like I pulled up a drowned man and hoped to revive him by warming him up, but I'm singing away. Some nights I'm so high I tend to neglect the rules of the road. The other night a freighter passed so close I saw the guy up in the pilot house, I saw him so close I'd recognize him in a crowd if I was ever to be in a crowd again. They don't see you way down there, your running lights are the farthest stars in the universe. Ilona," kissing her brow, "I'll tell you a dream. Not mine but my friend's, the one who stepped off the cliff. He used to go out on the boat with me, he used to help me out. One morning he comes up on deck—I'd been on watch while he slept—and he says, 'Oh, you still here?' And he told me he dreamed he woke up and came up on deck and I'm not there. Morning clear and brilliant, without me."

Lying close beside him, she knew he was telling her about his friend's dream to waken her even more to his presence, to the preciousness of his life.

Then, in the deceptive calm of strangers surprising themselves as lovers, "Ilona, tell me what you mean by blessed. Who is?"

So Martin had told him about that day she'd raved on and on, berserk. What Martin knew about her worst moments—shouldn't he have kept it secret out of respect for her, someone who appears to be balanced most of the time?

"My mind's way back in the Dark Ages."

He was stroking her hair, waiting just as Martin had waited, out in the sun and the wind. "The reason I asked, I thought if I was going to go around on that shelf every seven thousand years, maybe I'd be certified as blessed. I'd be remembered forever, more or less, and my picture was going to keep me the same age I was then, thirty and a good-looker. But what the hell. One day out of seven thousand years guarantees me nothing. I'm going to take that stuff down to the boat and throw it over. Something's bound to wash ashore. Somebody, say in Patagonia, is going to pick up a shoe and wonder who it belonged to. Did you know the ocean currents can take a shoe around the world? See, this guy's standing on this desolate shore, way down there, he's standing there with my shoe in his hand, thinking 'Who the hell did this belong to?' I like that idea. I could be anybody."

His hand stroking her face came to rest over her mouth, where no answer was waiting, nor any further speculation as to who was blessed and who was not.

"Ilona, you suffer from delusions of the other fellow's

153

grandeur. Whoever they may be—saints of all sorts, Nobel Prize winners, Jesus, Tolstoy, maybe Garbo, anybody in the hands of what *you* think is a great destiny. Ilona, I struggle with that delusion myself, all my life, and that's why I stay out there at night, because out there we're all in the same boat. I've got them all jammed into my smelly little boat that's going to spring a leak any minute. Ilona"—kissing her brow. "Come out with me some night."

When he fell asleep his hand slipped down from her mouth, his arm stretched out and his hand opened palm up.

# 23

Claud slept, and she lay listening to the waves breaking. She had never fallen asleep before the man beside her slept, and it had been that way with her child. She hadn't slept until the child slept. Long ago she had been charged to observe the drifting away of the spirit and just by her waking presence protect the sleeper in that transition. She slept, then. Startled awake, she lay waiting to learn just what it was that had waked her but it would not let itself be known. All she knew was that there was more space out in the heavens for it to swoop down and farther depths in the ocean for it to rise up and surge toward the ledge on which they lay.

She dressed in the room that faced the ocean and lit the lamp. The light would tell her where the house was when she made her way out from the waves. It would tell her where Claud was. His sleeping presence would guide her out just as Martin, without his knowing, had drawn his wife out from the ocean at his doorstep. The lights of earth are all the beings who draw you out from the dark, and are they everyone in your life?

One step down, and her bare feet sank into cold sand. The wind off the ocean snapped strands of hair across her eyes. She went down toward the water at a diagonal, struggling against the wind, wanting to give herself over—only for a moment—to that engulfing embrace, wanting to immerse herself in the element that was to wake her in the night, all the nights of that year, and after. Above the sound of deep water spunglass notes sprang up, almost like voices. Out before her now lay the vast surface glazed over by the stars' light. The ocean was a great eye, turbulent over its blindness.

Even in the cold sweep of the shallows there was such a merciless draw. The sand under her feet yielded to it and yielded her over. She stepped down the slope until the water rose to her breasts, and in that rocking expanse, in that rising mound before the first big wave broke, she turned and looked back to shore. The unlit houses along the sand were unseeable and the few lights were dimmed by the turmoil of distance and mist. The waters surging around her shifted her sight and jumbled the lights about and the light in the little house where Claud slept jumped sideways. The tremendous wave broke over her, knocking her under, dragging her down, and when she fought her way up and was almost standing again, the wave that followed struck her down again, and within that raging blindness she beat her way toward shore or toward where the shore was last seen.

"Ilona!"

Ilona. Her name came over the din like a stone skipped over a calm lake, and in that voice was an intensity of need for her presence on earth. Against the waters sweeping her back she found her footing and made her way toward the little figure, indistinct, running along the sand.

Design by David Bullen
Typeset in Mergenthaler Cloister
and Imprint by Wilsted & Taylor
Printed by Maple-Vail
on acid-free paper